Miss Sophia Nevill ~~~~~~~~~~~~~~~~~~~~ ~~e
heroines of her favou~~~~~~~~~~~~~~~~~~~~~~ *he
Prisoner of the Vampir~~~~~~~~~~~~~~~~~~~~g
stranger—*nor* forced ~~~~~~~~~~~~~~~~~~~~ ~~n~~!

When she encounter~~~~~~~~~~~~~~~~~~~~~~e,
Sophie feels sure that she has found her hero. Yet somehow,
life in the Polite World has a way of running contrary—not in
the least like the plots of her beloved stories. How can she be
sure that her own adventure will have the right happy ending?

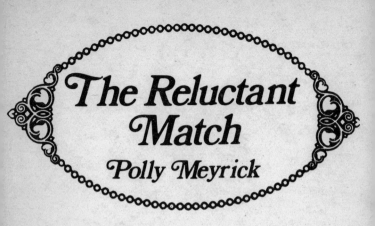

The Reluctant Match

Polly Meyrick

MILLS & BOON LIMITED
London · Sydney · Toronto

First published in Great Britain 1981
by Mills & Boon Limited, 15–16 Brook's Mews,
London W1A 1DR

© Polly Meyrick 1981
Australian copyright 1981
Philippine copyright 1981

ISBN 0 263 73438 2

Set in VIP Baskerville 10 on 11 pt by
Fakenham Press Limited

Made and printed in Great Britain by
Cox & Wyman Ltd., Reading

CHAPTER ONE

'THE wicked Count advanced upon Leonore smiling evilly. The terrified girl shrank back yet farther into the corner, her tender frame revolted in every cell. Inexorably her stepfather moved nearer till at last he seized her in his arms and pressed her close against his bosom. His dark eyes glittered down at her as her white face looked up into his.

"And now you shall be mine, my beauty," he cried, a sinister leer twisting his features. "I have waited long for you." And so saying, he fastened his savage lips to hers, bruising her mouth with the ferocity of his passion.

When at last the Count's iron arms relaxed a little, Leonore panted, "But sir, you are my stepfather!" . . . .'

Sophie shuddered with exquisite pleasure, and eased herself back on her heels. It was delightful to find a novel which so exactly reproduced her own situation in every way. Well—perhaps not quite *every* way, but certainly the coincidences were very remarkable. It was true she was not imprisoned in a haunted Transylvanian castle where vampires flew at night and ravished maidens' bodies were found daily in the moat, but—she *was* an orphan, and she *had* been left to the tender mercies of her stepfather, Mr Moreton, and though he had never been anything but kind to her, well, he *was* her stepfather and one could never be—well, step-parents did not have a very good reputation; and there *was* a lake at the bottom of the shrubbery, though all that was ever found floating there were a few fallen autumn leaves and the occasional expired goldfish. Still, the coincidences *were* very remarkable. Sophie read on.

'"No matter," Count Mannheim hissed. "First you shall be mine, *and then, when I have done with you, I shall marry you off to my good friend, the Baron Schwartzkopf."*

Leonore gasped and shuddered again. The Baron Schwartzkopf was an old man, as evil as her stepfather, but very, very rich, and famed for his unspeakable orgies.

"He will pay well for you, my little doe. He thrives upon the soft flesh of virgins, but we need not tell him. . . ."'

'Sophie, my dear. . . .'

The Prisoner of the Vampire fell to the floor with a thud as Sophie started and lifted her flushed face to look at her stepfather.

'Oh, sir, how you startled me!'

'I am sorry you had a fright, Sophie.' Oliver Moreton bent to pick up the fallen book and glanced at the title. 'Oh, Sophie, Sophie, no wonder you were frightened. Did you think the vampire had come upon you?' he asked with a whimsical smile.

Sophie blushed, but looked defiant. Her stepfather was always making fun of her novels. But did not they form a very fine guide to a young lady's life and conduct? And Sophie, barely seventeen and shortly to come out, was sure she could learn much from them. More than her governesses had been prepared to teach her, at all events! All they had seemed to think she needed to know were dreary things about stupid old Julius Caesar, who had not even bothered to find out about the English tides before trying to invade us, and even drearier things about squares and parallelograms, the angles of which, for some incomprehensible reason, apparently added up to a circle! Though what use that fact would be in life, Sophie quite failed to see. But if she were to make a success of her come-out, Sophie was quite certain she would have need of far different knowledge. And shut away in darkest Dorset without any mother to guide her, she would just have to prepare herself as well as she could.

She had always hoped, expected even, that Lady Hetherington, the mother of her great friend, Camilla, would invite her to accompany them to London for the Season. For it had always been established that that was where Camilla would make her come-out. The girls had often spoken of it the previous year, but now that the Season was nearly arrived, Camilla had not mentioned it again, and when Sophie had said once,

'Oh, Camilla, what fun it would be if we could come out together!'

Camilla had looked oddly embarrassed and had merely said with averted eyes, 'Oh, Sophie deawest, if only it could be so!' and had turned the conversation immediately to something else.

And a little while later, when Lady Hetherington had given a party for Camilla's seventeenth birthday and Sophie had not even been invited, Sophie had stormed at Camilla and shouted that she and all her family were quite horrid, and that she never wanted to see her or them again. She had not let Camilla get out one word and it was not till a day or two later, when Sophie called at Vale Court to apologise most meekly to her friend, that she learnt from Lady Hetherington herself the reason for the slight.

Camilla had tried to explain to her at first.

'But deawest Sophie, you know you are not quite seventeen, and you still have Miss Andwews, and Mamma is always so vewy particular about such things. You know she would not let me attend Belle's ball last year, for all there is but nine months and fifteen days between us!'

But later, as she was walking down a corridor at Vale Court, Sophie had overheard Lady Hetherington saying to a visitor,

'Simply can not depend upon her at all, my dear! We are likely to have a scene at the slightest provocation. So of course I have told Mr Moreton that the idea is quite impossible! *Quite* impossible! I am quite sorry about it, for I am fond of the child, and Camilla would be so happy to have her, but I could not possibly be responsible for introducing such a little virago. There really is no other word for it! From her father, you know. Dear Sophia Renton was calm as a mill-pond. How she came to marry that dreadful Henry Neville I could never understand. But there it is, I have told Mr Moreton that I simply dare not take her with us.'

Sophie had stopped and listened quite shamelessly. Her cheeks burnt with mortification and it was all she could do to hold her tears in check, and when she returned to Camilla she had been horrid to her once more and had left Vale Court in a temper.

It was shortly after this that Lady Hetherington announced that she was taking Camilla to London immediately in order to get her some more fashionable clothes than could be contrived by the dressmakers of Mallowfield. Sophie had been quite insufferable for two days, and it had ended in her final governess, Miss Andrews, giving her notice at last.

But it was very shortly after this that Sophie's grandmother, Lady Knight, had written to say that she was prepared to give a ball for her in June, and, to Sophie's delighted surprise, Mr Moreton had said he thought it would be an excellent thing for her, and had written back at once to accept the invitation.

His acceptance had been all the more astonishing in that Sophie knew full well that he did not wholly approve of Lady Knight. Sophie had not met her grandmother since she was quite young, but she knew she lived a very fashionable life in London, for her name was often mentioned in the newspapers as being present at routs and balls, and when these reports had appeared Sophie had seen Mr Moreton purse his lips and click his tongue disapprovingly. But Sophie read all such reports avidly, and thought how desirable her grandmother's life must be, and she longed for the day when mention might be made of Miss Sophie Neville as being present at some such evening gathering.

Now she looked up, frowning, at her stepfather, who was holding her book out to her.

'Thank you, sir,' she said somewhat ungraciously, as she took it.

'If you can spare the time, Sophie my dear, I would like to talk to you.' Mr Moreton's manner was unusually serious.

Seeing that she was not to be teased about *The Prisoner of the Vampire*, Sophie sat up obediently, folded her hands in her lap, and looked all attention. She could dwell upon Leonore's plight while her stepfather was talking.

Mr Moreton seated himself, and, leaning back, put the tips of his fingers together as he surveyed Sophie kindly.

In spite of herself, Sophie began to feel uncomfortable. Her stepfather was not often so formal, and she was sure there must be a reprimand coming. She wondered what it could be about. She wriggled a little under his scrutiny. Perhaps he had found out about her going in to Mallowfield and spending the whole of her month's allowance on that green velvet bonnet with the long, sweeping ostrich feather. In the shop window it had looked so romantic, and when she had tried it on she had fancied it made her look like the Archduchess Katarina in *The Sable Eagles of Karsova*. It had looked so dramatic, and Sophie had emptied her purse without a second's hesitation. But when she had put the bonnet on again at home, she did not like it near so much after all; in fact she had thought, appalled, that it made her look old, and so she had hidden it at the back of the toy cupboard in her old nursery.

But in spite of these thoughts, Sophie returned her stepfather's gaze without flinching. That particular month, Sophie was modelling herself on the Duchess of Taormina in *The Bells of the Sicilian Vespers* and the Duchess never flinched.

'Leonore gathered the shreds of her courage to her and faced her tormentor. She raised her chin proudly and addressed the Count contemptuously, disdain adding regality to her beautiful countenance.

"There is nothing you can do to me," she said calmly, "that will

force me to sign that document. Do your worst. Kill me if you will. But sign? Never!"

The Count's lips twisted into an ugly sneer.

"We shall see, my proud beauty, if you are so certain of yourself when you have passed a night in——"'

'Sophie!' Mr Moreton's voice sounded a little louder than usual. 'Sophie—are you listening to me, my dear?'

'Oh—oh yes, sir!'

'I was explaining, Sophie'—and here her stepfather gave a little sigh, as if doubting his ability to hold her attention for long. He had frequently thought it: she was in many ways similar to the lepidoptera which were his main interest in life: always flitting from one subject to another, never paying attention to anything for long, unless it was one of those circulating library novels which seemed to fill most of her waking hours. He sighed again. He had done his best for her, but somehow he must have gone wrong. She had none of her dear late mother's application to serious study. It was not that she was stupid—oh no! Really, she was quite intelligent.

It was true that she was able to play upon the pianoforte only moderately well, though she had a sweet, true voice, and she certainly had no talent for sewing or drawing or paper-cutting; her shell and seaweed pictures left much to be desired, though her mother might have valued them had she lived. But none of her many governesses had been able to instil any serious purpose into her. He supposed that it must be the common way with young ladies, but still—he had hoped she might take a small interest at least in some intellectual pursuit. But Sophie had no inclination for anything in the blue-stocking line.

Up to his marriage, Mr Moreton had led a wholly scholarly life, spending all his time in research for his great volume on the lepidoptera of the British Isles; and when, on his wife's demise, he had suddenly found himself the guardian of a headstrong female child, he had been somewhat at a loss. But he had shouldered the burden and done as well as he could.

Yes, Sophie was a dear child, unfortunately given to frittering away her time.

Her temper was her one serious defect, doubtless inherited, like her red hair, from her father. She was normally polite, but when her temper was roused—well, it was disturbing to say the least. True, she was always very contrite afterwards, and vowed to be better in the future, but one could never be quite sure what would set her off. Mr Moreton knew that he must tread carefully. He had funked it till now, preferring peace, and so he had left it almost too late.

Sophie waited for her stepfather to continue. He is getting old now, she thought as she looked at him; he must be nearly sixty. She had known him as long as she could remember, for her widowed mother had married again when she was a baby. She had always lived with him in the country and he had always kept a very quiet establishment, and there were few of the pleasures that young ladies delight in: no picnics, no impromptu parties, no gossip, no young men. Not that Sophie had been, or was, unhappy. She was merely looking forward to entering the social round at last.

'Now that you are shortly to come out, Sophie,' Mr Moreton had begun, 'I have been giving a great deal of thought to your future. As you know, I am your guardian till you come of age in four years' time, but I would be very glad to see you happily married long before that. Unfortunately, I am not able to provide for you as I and your dear mother would have wished. You know, I am sure, that this estate is entailed, and I have at my disposal only the yearly income which, though adequate for our needs now, does not permit me to give you the dowry I would like to provide for you.'

'You are very kind, sir, but I am not proposing to marry for a long time yet—at least six months—perhaps a little longer. So pray do not concern yourself prematurely now.' Sophie had been touched by her stepfather's concern, and spoke quite seriously.

'Six months, I collect, is not a long time in these matters,'

Mr Moreton answered without the flicker of a smile. 'I suppose that you—er—have not anyone in mind?'

Sophie shook her glossy ringlets. 'Oh, no. Not yet, sir.'

'I see. But even now that I know you have no *immediate* need of provision being made, I think we must discuss the matter. I am no longer a young man, and of late, as you know, my health has not been all that I might wish. I confess that I would like to see you settled, for unhappily you must realise, Sophie, that it is quite possible that you might suddenly find yourself without a roof over your head. It is my very distant cousin who will succeed me here, and as I have never met him, I do not know what character of man he is. So you will understand my anxiety to see you well settled now that you are grown up.'

'You are very good, sir,' said Sophie, much touched. 'And I assure you I will do my best to make a creditable match as soon as I possibly can. I will look about me as soon as I arrive at my grandmother's house. I know what a feather in my cap it would be to be engaged before the end of the Season.'

Mr Moreton had to hide his smile in a cough, but went on perfectly gravely.

'As I say, I have of late been giving the matter much thought. It is quite obvious to me that a young woman such as yourself—is at a—certain disadvantage—when it comes to choosing the lucky man upon whom she will bestow her favours. Here in Dorset we lead a very quiet life, and when you do go to London for your come-out, you will find a very great difference.' His kind eyes looked worriedly at Sophie for a moment. 'Your grandmother, Lady Knight, I fear leads an excessively—fashionable life. You will meet a great many —unusual—persons under her roof.'

Sophie looked at him, wondering what he could mean and thinking the answer might be interesting. But her stepfather did not elucidate. He continued:

'I gave a solemn promise to your dear mother upon her deathbed that I would make the best arrangements for your future that lay within my power. With this in mind, I have had some consultations with my old friend, Sir Llewellyn Godfrey. He is still much in the world—he was a very gay dog in his younger days. I remember once when we were up at Trinity he rode his horse up a staircase and into a party in Anthony Fanshawe's rooms—for a wager, you know, and—but there, all that is a long time ago.' And here Mr Moreton sighed, whether for his lost youth or some other cause was not clear.

'And what happened to the horse?' Sophie asked wide-eyed.

'I—I forget.'

'Oh, sir, you can not!'

'I—I think we gave it a bucket of champagne,' Mr More-ton answered vaguely.

'And then?'

'I seem to remember the animal went to sleep and could not be got out till the following morning.'

'Oh, sir!' said Sophie laughing.

Her stepfather jerked himself out of his reverie. 'As I was saying,' he resumed, this time more briskly, 'I have discussed the situation with my old friend. With very little trouble he thought of an answer to the problem, and so, after a great deal of thought, I entered into negotiations.'

'Negotiations?'

Mr Moreton nodded.

'Oh!' Sophie breathed, her heart beginning to beat some-what faster.

'I was so anxious to see you suitably settled—suitably provided for. I venture to think you will be pleased with what has been arranged.'

Now Sophie's heart really began to beat quickly. Surely—surely *The Prisoner of the Vampire* was not going to be an exact precursor of her own history! Surely her stepfather was not about to propose that she should marry his—his *old* friend—this—this Sir Llewellyn Godfrey!

'Yes, I do not think you will have any cause for complaint,' her stepfather continued with a trace of satisfaction in his voice. 'It would be very suitable indeed, and you would gain not only socially but also very materially by the match. I can not think why it did not occur to me. I own, I was quite delighted with the scheme.'

'I am not sure I understand you, sir,' Sophie said, dangerously quietly.

Now it must be remembered that Mr Moreton had been born in an age when arrangements such as those he was now about to outline were the usual thing, and it had not occurred to him that any very material changes in the custom had been brought about. He was fond of his stepdaughter, and he wished to do his duty by her for her own as well as for her dead mother's sake, and he had, as it happened, put himself out considerably in carrying out what he had thought to be right. He had put himself out so far, indeed, that he had missed a lecture at the Mallowfield Naturalists' Club by the eminent Oxford professor, Dr Featherton, a scholar Mr Moreton had been wanting to meet for several years, and the author of *The Lepidoptera of the Pyrenees*.

Remembering all this, he quite expected to be giving pleasure, and his own enthusiasm caused him to proceed less cautiously.

'I mean,' said Mr Moreton, his satisfaction now sounding very like smugness, 'that I have lighted upon an excellent partner for you. As I have said, his material circumstances leave nothing to be desired, and I do not think you will complain of his personal appearance—I am assured young females attach considerable importance to this, though what effect it can have upon a man's character and general suitability as a husband, I am at a loss to understand. But I assure you, *I* found him a very cheerful, well-mannered person, and I liked him immediately.'

'Did you, sir?' enquired Sophie, more quietly than ever. But Mr Moreton was too intent on his scheme.

'I have, of course, made the most extensive enquiries, though, of course, his connection with my old friend prejudiced me in his favour from the very start. I am quite convinced that you will like him, Sophie, and as I have said, I shall be greatly relieved when you are suitably settled.'

'Please let me understand you rightly, sir,' Sophie said slowly. 'Am I to understand that you are proposing that I should—*marry*—this—this connection of your old friend?'

'That is it exactly, Sophie,' exclaimed Mr Moreton with precipitate relief. 'I do not, of course, expect anything—immediate, you know. No immediate attachment, I mean. You will want to get to know the gentleman. But I certainly hope to see you betrothed before your come-out. That would obviate a great many—unfortunate—unpleasant—difficulties that I foresee arising from your residence with your grandmother, Lady Knight——'

'Betrothed before my come-out!'

'But on the other hand, I know that once engaged, young ladies may not wish to wait. A summer wedding is always pleasant, I think. Especially in the country.'

'A summer wedding! In the country!'

Mr Moreton nodded happily. His own wedding had been just such a one, in the little grey church filled with summer scabious and sweet marjoram.

'What—if I may ask, sir—is my—er—proposed suitor's name?' Sophie enquired with apparent meekness.

'His name is Netherton. Er—Michael Netherton.'

'And you think I should—marry—this—this Mr Michael Netherton?' Sophie pronounced the name with extreme distaste.

'He is not——' Mr Moreton began, but was cut short.

'Never!'

'I beg your pardon, Sophie?'

'I said "never"! I will not marry a stranger!' Sophie did her best not to shout, remembering even at such a time the damning words of Lady Hetherington.

'But he will not be a stranger. It is for the purpose of your becoming acquainted with him that I have asked him to wait upon us tomorrow afternoon at three o'clock.'

'Tomorrow! Oh!' And now Sophie stamped her foot with rage. 'You have actually asked him here tomorrow! Well, I tell you now, I will *never* marry this—this Mr Michael Netherfield, or whatever his name is! Never! A summer wedding! Betrothed before my come-out! Oh, how can you think of it?'

'But my dear Sophie, I am thinking of what is best for you! In my young days, young ladies were glad when early marriages were arranged for them. I would have thought—I mean, it is not as if you have——'

'But times have changed! We are living in the nineteenth century now!'

'When you meet the gentleman tomorrow, I am sure your opinion will change.'

'Never! Never! Never! I will *not* marry someone chosen for me!'

'But Sophie, my dear, how can you choose for yourself? How many young men do you know?'

'That is the reason for my come-out! For the ball my grandmamma Lady Knight will give for me! I shall meet them at my ball!'

Mr Moreton sighed. Things had clearly gone very wrong. 'But Sophie, my dear,' he protested gently, 'I have already tried to explain to you the advantages of being betrothed when you first go to London. If you are already suitably betrothed when you enter Society, the danger presented by the unsuitable acquaintances you will surely make will be eliminated.'

'And I suppose you would call it "suitable" that I should marry your old family friend!'

'It is an excellent match, my dear!'

'And this—this Mr Netherborne—I will wager this Mr Netherborne is older than I am!'

'Netherton. He is somewhat in advance of your years, certainly.'

'I knew it! I knew it! You are trying to marry me off to an old man!' Sophie almost jumped with rage, her face flaming. 'I am sure my mother would never have wished this for me. She would never have thought that you would behave exactly like—like Count Mannheim! Oh, you tried to stop me reading about him, and now I know why! Oh! How can you be so horrid! Well, I will not do it! I will never do it! Never! Never! Never!'

And with cheeks as red as her hair, and certain that she was sweeping from the room in the exact manner of the Duchess of Taormina, Sophie slammed the door behind her and sped up to her old nursery at the top of the house and locked the door.

She heard her stepfather's slow tread upon the staircase, and his anxious voice calling, 'Sophie! Wait! Listen to me!'

Sophie stood in the middle of the room, her hands over her ears.

'Sophie, my dear, please let me in,' Mr Moreton said in a reasonable tone, trying the handle of the door in vain. 'Let us discuss this in a sensible fashion.'

'I won't! I won't!' Sophie cried, stamping her foot and making her red curls shake vigorously. 'I won't marry an old man and it is unkind of you to suggest it!'

'But Sophie—you do not *have* to marry him—it is a suggestion, merely——'

'I am not listening! I cannot hear what you say! I will not listen! You may talk as long as you like, but I will never listen! And I will never marry your old friend!' Sophie shouted, her hands still over her ears.

From previous experience, Mr Moreton knew that there was no point in trying to reason with her when she was in a tantrum. He must wait till she had calmed down. He sighed mildly, and retraced his steps downstairs.

'Leonore listened to the sound of the satanic count's retreating footsteps echoing hollowly along the cavernous vaults. Fearfully she gazed round her noisome prison. By the light of the guttering taper she could see the slimy walls across which sidled nameless creatures of infinite horror. With growing despair she looked for a window, but there was none; the only exit was via the iron door through which she had lately entered, now securely locked and immovable against her frantic fingers.

Suddenly her blood ran cold, and she froze with terror. Something had moved in the murk, and the next moment a mocking, mirthless laugh assailed her ears. The thin taper dropped from Leonore's nerveless hand and was extinguished in the fall. In midnight blackness she waited, petrified, for the laugh to come again. Something brushed against her hair and with a low cry Leonore, unable to endure more, sank to the ground, senseless.'

It was exactly the same! Here she was, locked in a prison! True, she had locked herself in, and far from the slimy walls and nameless horrors of Leonore's dungeon, she was in her own old nursery, filled with the loved toys of her childhood. There were bars, it was true, to prevent escapes, but only on the lower part of the window, put there for the safety of young children, and in any case, no insuperable barrier, for once Sophie had scrambled out of the window and climbed down to the ground, clinging to the ivy which covered that wall of the house. But that had been three years ago, and now she shuddered as she looked down from the great height of the second storey.

Sophie sat down on the window-seat and kicked her heels against it. She would never—no—*never* marry this—this Mr Netheringham. She could just imagine him—old, wizened, bent, with soup-stains down his waistcoat and thin grey locks scattered sparsely on his bald pate. He might even still wear a wig! And he would hang it on a hook each night!

Sophie shivered with disgust, and to divert her attention

from the horrid picture, she began to think about the interesting young man she had seen in church the previous Sunday. Now *he* was all that a hero should be: tall, handsome, with dark brown hair and the most lively blue eyes. At least, Sophie thought they were blue. He had sat quite alone in one of the free pews, but quite clearly from his clothes and his bearing he was a gentleman. He appeared to be about one and twenty—just the ideal age. If only *he* would come and rescue her now! She would gladly marry him, she was quite sure.

Sophie sighed. It was a great pity, but there was no likelihood at all of his coming to rescue her. Why, she did not even know his name nor where he came from, and she was certain he could not know anything of her. She would have to manage alone.

But—she was determined never even to meet the odious Mr Netherwell. Quite, quite determined. There was only one thing to do and that was to leave Mallowfield. But—where should she go? She sighed again. She had no choice. She would have to go to Portland Square in London to her grandmother, Lady Knight. Rather earlier than had been arranged, but there was no help for it. Only one minor problem remained: how should she get there?

CHAPTER
TWO

THESE, then, were the events which resulted in Sophie later that same day sitting beside Jack Bean, the carter, as he made his slow journey from Mallowfield to London. Sophie had tried to get a seat in the stagecoach, promising that her grandmother, Lady Knight of Portland Square, would pay the fare when they reached the capital; but the guard would have none of it. Now Sophie regretted more than ever the purchase of the green velvet bonnet with the sweeping ostrich feather, and she had had a hard time persuading Jack to let her travel with him. But there she sat, her legs dangling over the edge of the cart, wearing that same green bonnet, her head held very high as she tried to reassure herself that she was doing the right thing.

'Leonore glanced covertly at the driver. The man's face was shadowed by the brim of his hat and the high collar of his travelling cloak hid much of his face. He had seemed honest enough, and Leonore had been thankful to accept his offer. Anything—anything—to take her farther away from her terrible prison. She must needs trust him. And yet there was something about him which caused her unease. Was it his preternaturally white skin? His strange, glowing eyes? His unblinking gaze? Leonore tried to still her fears, but she wished he would not whip up the horses to such a furious gallop. She clung to the side of the carriage, fearful of being thrown out, but it was only when they passed a brazier burning at the entrance to a bridge that she saw the driver's face clearly for the first time—and then she nearly swooned from terror. For it was not a face which she had seen illuminated by the passing flames, but a ghastly, fleshless skull.'

Sophie glanced hurriedly at Jack Bean's face to reassure

herself that she was not being driven by some unearthly ghost, and she felt considerably relieved as she looked at his weatherbeaten face, and saw his gnarled hands on the reins. In fact there was really only one thing which she could complain of: the pace was so agonisingly slow. The heavy work-horse plodded along, and Sophie watched with envious eyes as smart phaetons and curricles dashed by with their fashionable occupants. How she longed to be in such an elegant, fast equipage! Arriving on a cart was hardly the most refined way to enter London, but it could not be helped.

At the outset, she had feared that her stepfather would come after her to catch her and carry her, screaming, back to Mallowfield and the abominable Mr Netherset. Each vehicle she heard approaching from behind caused her to lower her head, and try to hide herself behind the carter's lean form, but as the hours passed, and there was no sign of Mr More-ton, she felt the danger of pursuit fade. Her resulting ease of mind was cancelled by the affront she felt at being so lightly lost. The Duchess of Taormina had not been allowed to escape so easily.

When it began to grow dark, however, Sophie suffered her first real misgivings, and she thought longingly of the dinner she might be eating at home. She had brought no luggage with her, carrying merely her reticule in which reposed a lace handkerchief, her mother's ring, and a new sovereign which she meant to spend upon food on the journey. The only other possession with her, apart from the clothes she stood up in, was her precious copy of *The Prisoner of the Vampire*. She grew uncomfortably certain that a roasted hindquarter of pork or some beef with oyster sauce would be of more use to her now.

She had never been out so long or so late alone before; now, here she was embarked upon a journey to London, without money enough to make sure that the journey was even toler-ably comfortable. Really, she should never have come! Where would they stop for the night? She must not spend all her sovereign at once at the beginning of the journey, for at this pace it would take many days, and how should she manage at the end if she were completely penniless?

Tears of self-pity pricked Sophie's eyes, but she forced them back, straightened her shoulders and determined to go on. She could not give up now, creep back ignominiously to her stepfather's house and marry the horrid Mr Netherwold. Thoughts of her fate if she returned to Mallowfield quickly fortified her. No, no! There was nothing to do but go forward.

At length the carter drew up at a small inn, and Sophie jumped down, glad to stretch her legs. Her heart sank as she saw what type of place it was: a poor hostelry with doubtless no comforts for a lady. But at least she might procure a cheap bed in such a place. With her head held high, but with trembling heart, she walked in and demanded to know if she could be accommodated. She was assured civilly that a room could be prepared for her, and she was shown into a small eating-room to wait for her meal. Meanwhile Jack Bean went off to the snug, and Sophie was left to ponder her situation alone.

But she cheered up very much when she saw that the meal brought to her was plain but wholesome. She ate ravenously, dispatched the whole quickly, and felt still better. Then she was shown to a tiny, but scrupulously clean room. Thankfully, she washed her face, took off her dress and went to bed in her chemise and fell asleep almost at once. She had only just time to remember a passage from *The Prisoner of the Vampire* before she closed her eyes.

'Leonore, near to death from weariness, dragged her tired limbs to the festering straw mattress and collapsed upon it, exhausted by terror and her own exertions. But blessed sleep did not steal over her with its balm of oblivion. She stretched out in the darkness, no more at rest than when she had been upright, petrified by the scufflings of the rats and the strange, unearthly noises which creaked through the old house.'

But no such fears troubled Sophie. If there were rats abroad, or supernatural presences made the floorboards creak in the depths of the night, she was oblivious of them. She woke refreshed at sunrise the following morning, in time to eat a hearty breakfast before Jack Bean was ready for the road.

At first she was quite, quite certain that Nemesis would overtake her today, and she was sure that every carriage which approached from behind must contain her stepfather, intent upon dragging her back to Mallowfield and the odious Mr Netherwell. But as time went by, and nothing happened to trouble her, she ceased to turn her head aside each time a carriage came abreast of them; disguised by the sweeping feather of the green bonnet, she felt safe and began to look about her with pleasure.

It was another day of brilliant sunshine, and at first Sophie quite enjoyed the regular rumbling of the cart's wheels as it trundled over the road, newly surfaced according to the specifications of the clever Mr McAdam. But before long, the slowness of the pace grew exceedingly irksome. She tried jumping from the cart and walking beside it to stretch her legs. Sometimes she walked on ahead and then sat down on the springy turf to wait for the cart to catch her up. Once she found a carpet of wild strawberries and stopped to pick them. She took so long over it that the cart was quite out of sight, and she had to run quite hard to catch up with it. And in the late morning, for a change, she sat at the back of the cart, dangling her legs over the edge and trying to read her book.

But it had turned out to be extremely unpleasant, for an exceedingly smart phaeton, instead of passing the cart, suddenly slowed down and the driver endeavoured to engage Sophie in conversation. Sophie was unutterably shocked. Never had she realised that a man might address a female in such particularly familiar terms. At first she had tried to ignore him, but when the man called her by some insolently improper endearments, and suggested that she might like to accompany him to indulge in what he termed 'a jollier frolic than sitting behind a knock-kneed, one-eyed nag', it was all

Sophie could do not to throw her book at her persecutor. But instead, she closed it with a bang, glared at the man angrily, and jumping off the cart, hurried forward to sit beside the protecting form of Jack Bean once more. The man in the phaeton laughed and kept turning round to wink at her till he rounded a corner and was out of sight.

The inn at which they stopped that night was somewhat larger than the hostelry of the previous evening. There were several travellers outside who eyed her curiously as she got down from the cart, and Sophie felt sadly dishevelled as she entered the building. She had noticed several very smart equipages in the inn yard, and inside the inn itself there was a group of very fashionably-dressed young women who looked askance at Sophie as she passed them. She wished very much that she had some party she might join, and a wave of furious anger washed over her as immediately she had passed the young ladies, she heard whispers and giggles which she was certain were directed at her.

Her cheeks flamed to the colour of her hair, and tears of fury jumped into her eyes. She wanted to shout at them that she was not normally so unkempt; that this was the first time she had ever been out unaccompanied; for she had recognised that in other circumstances, these girls were just the sort with whom she might have been friends. But now she could do nothing but toss the long green feather impatiently, and wait till she was attended to.

The arrival of the cart had coincided with the arrival of a coach, and Sophie was deliberately left to wait till all its passengers had been accommodated. It was while she was waiting that she saw a familiar face descending the staircase and she hurriedly turned away. It was the young man she had seen in church. How very unfortunate that he should be in this very inn! Out of all the hostelries in the country that he might have chosen! If only she did not look so bedraggled! She kept her back turned to him for some time until she was sure he must be out of sight, and then she ventured to peep round. But he was still there. He was standing by a window and turning over the pages of a newspaper. He really did look exceedingly handsome! She had not been mistaken in the impression she had formed in church. Her quick glance was sufficient to show her that the young ladies too were also not unobservant of his presence.

Sophie turned back to the innkeeper's wife, and at last the woman condescended to attend to her. She looked at Sophie with a supercilious air, and though this angered Sophie and she was tempted to put the woman in her place, she did not want to draw attention to herself, so she merely said in little more than a hiss:

'I want the best room you have in the house.'

'The best rooms are all taken by the Quality,' the woman replied insolently, with a glance at the group behind Sophie. 'All I have left is an attic room—but that is fit enough for the likes of you.'

Sophie gasped with indignation. Never, never had she been so spoken to before. She, Miss Neville, of Mallowfield House, to be addressed thus by a country innkeeper's wife!

'*And* I want to see the colour of your money first,' the woman went on.

'You are insolent!' Sophie breathed furiously. Oh, why was she subjected to this? It was all so distressingly like Leonore's experience at the inn near the river. Innkeepers, it seemed, did not take kindly to young females travelling alone without luggage. And now, what made it all the worse was that she was certain that the young ladies behind her were all listening to this conversation as hard as they could, and perhaps the unknown young man was too!

'Suit yourself, miss,' the woman said. 'Money first or no room.'

Sophie looked at her in baffled rage. If only there had been somewhere else to go; but she could not, even to escape this situation, contemplate spending the night in the open under a hedge! With flaming cheeks and a ferocious scowl she pulled open her reticule and put in her hand to take out her precious money.

'May I be of service, ma'am?' a man's voice beside her said suddenly.

Sophie turned her head and saw the young man she had seen in Mallowfield church bowing to her.

'Oh, it is you!' she exclaimed, and smiled with pleasure.

'Michael Fanshawe at your service, ma'am. I was not certain that you would remember me.'

'Oh, but of course I do!' Sophie said eagerly, without thinking.

'You are having difficulty with a room, I collect?' he went on, and turning to the innkeeper's wife he said, 'I do not think the attic room you offered this young lady quite adequate, do you?' He smiled at the woman, but his voice had a touch of steel in it.

'I am very sorry, I'm sure, sir, but we are so very busy, there is not one good room left in the house. Indeed, indeed, they have all been taken up,' and here she glanced again at the group of young ladies behind Sophie, who were pretending not to listen. 'And I am very sorry, sir, but I meant no harm, ma'am. But what is a poor body to do?'

'In that case,' Mr Fanshawe said smoothly, 'would you do me the honour of taking my room? I think you will find it comfortable—a great deal more comfortable than an attic room at all events.'

'You are indeed kind, sir!' cried Sophie. 'But I could not accept it. You must be tired——'

'And how could I possibly show my face again in Mallowfield if you do not accept it, ma'am? Do not, I beg you, put me into such an impossible situation. I much enjoyed my visit, and I would like to return.' He smiled down at Sophie as he spoke, and she could not help herself smiling back.

'It is really very kind, but——'

'That is all settled then,' said Mr Fanshawe comfortably, and turning to their hostess, he added, 'Have the lady's portmanteau taken to my room, if you please, and remove my own valise.'

'I—I do not have any portmanteau,' Sophie managed to gasp, blushing and feeling very uncomfortable.

'Oh, so it was *you* who had that accident on Chapel Hill, was it, ma'am? I am so very sorry. A nasty business. *Two* of the horses injured, I believe! *And* a broken wheel! It must have hindered you very greatly. But I dare say the lack of your portmanteau can be remedied for this evening, can not it, Mistress Biddle?'

'Oh yes, sir! Of course, sir! If you will come with me, ma'am, I will see to it.'

And the woman moved forward and then waited for Sophie to precede her.

Not knowing quite what to do, Sophie gave Mr Fanshawe a helpless, grateful smile, and walked up the oak staircase.

The room into which she was shown was a fine large one with a four-poster bed hung with crimson damask draperies, and covered by a handsome patchwork quilt. A wide bow window gave on to the road at the front of the inn, and an elegant sofa was placed in a convenient position to take advantage of the view.

Sophie's first reaction was one of pleasure that she would pass the night in such comfortable circumstances, but her next thoughts were far less cheerful. How could she possibly pay for such a room and a meal and still have money enough left for the rest of the journey?

The innkeeper's wife now stood smiling—it seemed to Sophie—somewhat unctuously. Sophie remembered the Duchess and the woman's previous treatment of her, and did not smile in reply.

'I will send up the boy directly to remove the gentleman's valise, ma'am. And what will you be taking for supper, ma'am? We have a fine dressed chicken, and some cold beef and oyster pie which will melt in the mouth. I can send up a very fine tray for you, ma'am.'

'Thank you, but that will not be necessary,' said Sophie loftily. 'I shall be dining in the eating-room.'

Sophie knew that she must speak to Mr Fanshawe without delay. It would be extremely embarrassing, but she must explain at once that she could not afford to stay in such a room, and that she had better take the one originally offered.

Sophie did not quite like the woman's smirk as she left the room. She was still contemplating this when there was a knock at the door, and the boots came in in answer to her reply.

'Stay,' Sophie commanded, as the boy bent down to pick up the valise.

It really was all exceedingly awkward. She had no idea what she ought to do. In none of the novels she had read had there ever been any heroine in a situation even remotely resembling this one. None of them had ever been in immediate need of money. They had been poor, some of them, yes, but they had never been called upon to disburse hard coin. Mostly they spent their time in haunted castles and horrid dungeons, and any food they had was provided free.

'You had better carry on,' she said at length, with a sigh. After all, the valise could always be brought back again.

The boy looked in the wardrobe and took out Mr Fanshawe's travelling coat and his hat. He picked up the silver-backed hairbrushes from the chest and stowed them in the valise. Meanwhile, Sophie went to the window and looked out. There was still a bustle of arrivals outside, and in the light from the flares Sophie noticed what appeared to be a very fine curricle drawn by a pair of matched chestnuts. There seemed to be a crest painted on the side of the vehicle, surmounted by an earl's coronet. Sophie watched with even more interest when she saw Mr Fanshawe come out of the inn, and walk across to speak to the groom leading the horses.

At that moment there was another knock at the door, and Sophie turned from the window and called 'Come in.'

A maid appeared in the doorway bearing a flannel night-gown, a comb and some washing cloths.

'Mistress Biddle's compliments, miss, and she says as 'ow she 'opes they will be suitable, miss.'

'Thank you. I am sure they will do very well. Please thank Mrs Biddle.'

The maid bobbed a curtsy and set the items down, then left the room after giving another curtsy.

Sophie went over to inspect the nightgown. She held it against her; it was a little long, but it was trimmed with good lace, and Sophie reflected, a little puzzled, on the change that there had been in her treatment since Mr Fanshawe had spoken to her. It had been very lucky that he had been there and had remembered her. She thought uneasily of what might have happened if he had not come to her aid. But she still had to pay for the night, and—well, it was all very difficult.

With a sigh, she took off her bonnet with the ostrich feather which had been responsible for her reduction in circum-stances, and combed her red curls into some semblance of order. She washed her face, and suddenly felt ravenously hungry. So, smoothing her sleeves and picking up her reticule, she made her way downstairs.

She was disappointed not to see Mr Fanshawe in the hall, so she peeped into the eating-room but saw that he was not there either. She picked up a newspaper and made a pretence of reading it, but when after some minutes there was still no sign of Mr Fanshawe, she began to feel alarmed. She started when a waiter approached her.

'Mr Fanshawe's compliments, ma'am, and would you be pleased to eat now? Supper has been laid in this room over here.'

'Oh, thank you,' cried Sophie, much relieved, and turned to follow the waiter. It was only then that the impropriety of dining alone in a private room with Mr Fanshawe struck her. She hesitated, but followed the waiter and entered the room. It was quite a small apartment, and inside there was a table laid for one.

'Is Mr Fanshawe——?' she began.

'Mr Fanshawe has already gone, ma'am. It was quite unexpected, but he had a sudden change of plan. Shall I serve the soup now, ma'am?'

Feeling exceedingly alarmed, Sophie sat down and unfolded her napkin and watched the waiter serve the soup. If Mr Fanshawe were no longer in the inn, she was in an even more unhappy situation, and she felt a slight irritation that he had let her down. She was only in this mess because of him! She could perfectly well have had the attic room, uncomfortable as it would undoubtedly have been. It was too bad of him!

But the food placed before her was quite delicious, and in spite of her misgivings, Sophie ate with a will. And by the time she had finished the soup and the chicken, and the ham, and the portion of steak and oyster pie, and a large slice of peach and strawberry tart with sugar flowers and angelica sticks, she had decided that there was nothing for it but to pay the bill on the morrow, and be stringently economical for the rest of the journey. It would be too humiliating to go to Mrs Biddle and ask to change her room now. She could only hope for the best.

Sophie was by nature optimistic, and having decided this, she put the matter out of her mind. She returned to her comfortable room, prepared herself for the night, climbed into the big bed and slept soundly, having been able to keep her eyes open only long enough to learn that Leonore escaped from her current prison by the aid of a mysterious masked stranger.

The following morning, after she had breakfasted, she

demanded the bill, only to be told that all had been settled by Mr Fanshawe before he left.

'Did—did he say where he was travelling?' Sophie asked immediately, without thinking of the impression she might be giving.

'He said something about the Golden Pheasant at Nether Belton, I understand, miss.'

'But after that?'

'I do not know, miss.'

The carter was somewhat surprised that his passenger did not chatter away as usual that morning. But Sophie was puzzling over Mr Fanshawe, and though she was, of course, very grateful to him indeed, she felt somehow that she had been placed in an awkward situation. Was she irrevocably compromised in having accepted board and lodging from him? She had not asked for it—but then, neither had it been forced upon her. She made up her mind that if ever she saw Mr Fanshawe again, she must repay the debt.

She looked out for him expectantly that evening when they stopped, but there was no sign of him. Nor did he appear the next evening, and Sophie felt unreasonably disappointed. She told herself crossly that she was foolish in expecting to see him. He would long ago have finished *his* journey, and there was no likelihood at all of his reappearing. Nevertheless, she felt let down. Still, she reflected the following morning as the cart moved slowly on its way through Hampshire, perhaps it was just as well. She had become quite accustomed to sleeping in her chemise, and her dress was still quite reasonable, for when they had been caught in a sharp summer shower, the carter had put a sack round her shoulders, and that had kept off the worst of the rain.

But her velvet bonnet was a different matter. It had become sadly spotted, and the feather was no longer fluffy and upright. Now it seemed to hang dejectedly over one ear, not at all in the fashion of the Archduchess Katarina, who had never had to be protected by sacking, and in the end

Sophie pulled it off and dropped it in a hedgebottom. Her bonnet might look untrimmed now, but at least it was no longer ridiculous.

But truth to tell, Sophie would have been very glad to sleep in her own bed again. Even the thought of Mr Michael Netherton was not so dreadful as it had once been. She mused on the fact that both Mr Fanshawe and Mr Netherton had the same Christian name. If only it had been Mr Fanshawe and not—— But Sophie stopped this profitless speculation. She only hoped that she would meet someone as nice as Mr Fanshawe once she was arrived in London.

At the end of another long and tedious day, the carter turned into an inn yard. Now they were nearer London, there was much more traffic, and there were so many vehicles outside the Red Lion that Sophie feared there would be no room for them.

'Would not it be better to try another inn, Jack? I have never seen so many carriages together before.'

'Oi allus stop yer, Miss Sophie. The 'oss can't go no further, and noither can Oi.'

'I just wonder if there will be room for us.'

'Oi nivver 'ave no trouble o' that.'

'Do they keep a room for you then, Jack?'

'Maybe. But then if they'm full, Oi sleeps in the 'ay-loft.'

'Oh!' Sophie said blankly. That had not occurred to her. As she got down from the cart, she reflected that she might be reduced to it yet. There were at least three more nights to go before they were in London.

As she walked across the yard, she thought she noticed something familiar about one of the grooms. He walked over to a smart curricle, and she saw it was harnessed to a fine pair of matched chestnuts. Surely it was the one she had seen at the inn three nights ago? Yes! There was the earl's coronet on the side panel. If only it could have been Mr Fanshawe instead! Though there would have been little point in it, for she had not money to repay him now.

She walked into the inn, very conscious of her dishevelled appearance. She thought people glanced at her curiously as she walked by them, and she would have given a good deal to look as she normally did when her maid had finished dressing her. She had to wait till the innkeeper was free to serve her, and then she asked to be accommodated in a small room. The man looked at her very doubtfully, but his glance had the effect of stiffening Sophie's manner. Even if she did look more like a penurious governess than a young lady, she was still Miss Neville of Mallowfield, and accustomed to deference. She stared back at him imperiously, and the man's eyes appeared to waver for a moment, but then his wary expression reappeared, and Sophie was certain that she was to be subjected to some impertinent remark when a familiar voice said,

'Why, Miss Neville! What a delightful surprise!'

Sophie turned swiftly and found the amused eyes and smiling face of Mr Fanshawe gazing down at her.

CHAPTER
THREE

'Oh, Mr Fanshawe! How you startled me!'

'I beg your pardon, ma'am. But—er—I am correct in thinking that there is some difficulty about a room?' The corners of his eyes creased delightfully, and his smile broadened a little.

'I am not sure,' returned Sophie with becoming dignity, and turning to the innkeeper, she gazed at him interrogatively.

'Oh, certainly, miss,' the man said hastily. 'Certainly. We do have one room left.'

'Is it a *small* room?' Sophie insisted.

The man's eyes wavered to meet Mr Fanshawe's and then returned to Sophie's face. 'It—it is at the side, miss, but I am sure you will find it comfortable. We are so busy, miss—sir, but it *is* very comfortable——'

'So long as it is a small room——'

Again the man's eyes wavered to Mr Fanshawe's face before he replied.

'I think you will find it suitable, miss.'

'Very well. I will take it.'

And then Sophie turned to Mr Fanshawe.

'If I could detain you for a few moments, Mr Fanshawe, I would very much like to speak with you.'

'Why certainly, ma'am. I am quite at your disposal.'

'Perhaps—if you do not mind—we might take a turn outside? It is still quite light.'

'At your service, ma'am,' Mr Fanshawe said, bowing.

Sophie walked out through the front door and away from

the bustle of the carriages and other travellers. She saw that the coroneted curricle was still at the inn door.

'Mr Fanshawe,' she began, when they were a little apart, 'how did you know my name?'

'Did not you tell it me?' he answered promptly.

'I do not think so.' Sophie was doubtful.

'Then I must have heard it in Mallowfield. Yes, that must be it. I remember asking who you were. I hope you do not mind,' he said, turning his strong blue eyes full upon her face.

'Oh—no! No, of course not. I only wondered——' That must be it, certainly, though—— But there was a more important matter to settle first, and Sophie began again. 'Mr Fanshawe—I will be frank with you. I—I find myself in a very difficult position. I—must repay you—for your kindness in giving up your room to me the other night, but unfortunately——'

Here she came to a halt. She was, in any case, quite unaccustomed to conversing with young men—had certainly—in her life—never conversed alone with one before—and as for talking about money! Why, never before had she even had to consider her financial situation! Not for such necessities as food and lodging, at all events. Whether she should buy a new pair of gloves or a fresh silk ribbon had been the hardest decision she had yet had to make in that line. And discussing such expenditure with Camilla was no help now. They were both kept on fairly small allowances, and many was the complaint they had made to each other about the difficulty of managing on such a paltry sum as they received! But never!—never! had they had to consider purchasing the needs of life. Sophie diverted her train of speech.

'Of whom did you ask my name, Mr Fanshawe? You were staying in Mallowfield, I collect?'

'No, no. Not *in* Mallowfield. I was—er—staying in the neighbourhood.'

'Oh! You see, Mr Fanshawe,' Sophie went on, 'I—er, I am

not yet——' She had been about to say that she was not yet out, but considering her present circumstances she thought better of it. 'I—I lead a very—quiet life there. I do not have a very great acquaintance.'

'I see,' he answered gravely. 'But you surprise me, Miss Neville. I would have thought otherwise.'

Sophie glanced into his face, but quickly turned away her head. She did not quite understand his look, and felt embarrassed for a reason she could not have explained. To hide her feelings, she tossed her head and continued,

'As I was saying, Mr Fanshawe, I find myself in an exceedingly—difficult—situation. Owing to certain—er—circumstances, I find myself from home—without—er—sufficient money to repay you for my lodging the other night.' She finished in a hurry, blushing dreadfully.

'Please let us say no more about it, Miss Neville,' Mr Fanshawe urged. 'When your—circumstances—are recovered, then we may talk about it.'

'You are very kind, sir,' said Sophie gratefully. 'But I must insist that you allow me to repay you when I am able. I am at this moment journeying to my grandmother, Lady Knight of Portland Square, and I must beg you to wait upon me there so that I may cancel my debt,' she finished, not quite daring to look up into his face.

'I shall be delighted to do so, Miss Neville.'

'That is—' Sophie said awkwardly, 'I think I shall be staying with my grandmother, but she does not as yet know—that I am coming.'

'Are you travelling quite alone, Miss Neville?' Suddenly Mr Fanshawe spoke quite firmly. 'Oh, I do not wish to pry into your concerns,' he went on hastily, 'but it seems to me that you are in need of help. I mean—you are quite without portmanteaux—and you have no maid with you——'

'It is very kind of you to be so concerned, sir, but I am able to manage very well——'

'But perhaps a little help would not come amiss——?'

His voice sounded so kind, and there was so much concern in his blue eyes, that Sophie impulsively decided to confide in him.

'Oh, Mr Fanshawe, I am indeed in great need! I am a most unfortunate being, but—but—I was not able to do otherwise.'

'Otherwise than what, Miss Neville?'

'Mr Fanshawe, I will be frank with you. I am running away from my stepfather.'

'Running away!'

Sophie nodded vigorously.

'But—may I ask why, pray?'

'You may indeed!' Sophie said warmly. 'My stepfather wishes me to become betrothed to—an old man!'

'An old man!' exclaimed Mr Fanshawe blankly.

Sophie nodded more vigorously than ever. 'Yes! Is not it truly dreadful? I was so overcome when he informed me of his wishes, and then—on top of that—to tell me that—this— this person was to wait upon me the very next day! Oh! I assure you, I nearly fainted with horror!'

And here Sophie looked up into Mr Fanshawe's face. 'And that is why I ran away in a great hurry, and have no luggage, nor money enough with me to repay you at this moment. But you will oblige me very much if at some convenient time, you will call upon me in Portland Square, and then all can be settled. I do not suppose I shall be there before next week, for my conveyance is exceedingly slow, and had I known what it would be like I should have endeavoured to make better preparations before setting out. But all I could think of was to escape from the fate worse than death my stepfather was preparing for me!' Sophie finished dramatically.

'Miss Neville! Miss Neville! I see you are indeed in sad straits. But pray, do not think any more about—pray do not mention any debt. And as for your conveyance, it would give me the greatest pleasure—the very greatest pleasure in the world, I assure you, to convey you myself to your grandmother's, Lady Knight's, or wherever else you may wish!' And he smiled down at her in a very particular way with his astonishingly blue eyes.

'That is very kind, sir,' returned Sophie, somewhat flustered, 'but I could not accept so much from—from a—stranger.'

'Oh, pray do not say that, Miss Neville. We are not quite strangers, surely! Can not we consider ourselves at least a little acquainted?'

Sophie could not resist smiling up at him. Really, Mr Fanshawe had the most—charming—way of putting things.

'That would be delightful, Mr Fanshawe, but—well, it would not be quite *true*, would it? At least, we *may* be acquainted, but I am not at all sure we should be, for we have never been introduced!'

Mr Fanshawe frowned. 'I see the difficulty,' he said gravely. 'Now, let me see. We must have some mutual acquaintance. I feel sure we must have some.'

'You said you were staying in the neighbourhood of Mallowfield——' Sophie prompted.

'When I enquired your name.' Mr Fanshawe smiled down at her again. 'Yes, I was staying with my friend Barton of Hopewell Hall. But I attended Mallowfield church because I do not care for the sermons of the Hopewell incumbent. I attended one Sunday, but did not care to repeat the experience. I have never been more wearied in my life.'

'Oh, Mr Fenton is a very well-known Evangelical,' Sophie said, smiling. 'He is famous for his sermons, though I am glad to say I have never heard one. But did you say you were staying at Hopewell Hall?'

'Yes.'

'Then you know Lord Barton. My stepfather is often with him. They are on the Bench together.'

'Then everything is all right, Miss Neville,' Mr Fanshawe said gladly. 'I have known Barton for many years, and if he is

acquainted with your stepfather, then I *might* have met him
while I was at Hopewell. What is your stepfather's name—it
is not Neville, I collect?'

'No. He is a Mr Oliver Moreton.'

'Moreton. Moreton,' repeated Mr Fanshawe, consider-
ingly. 'I think I might have heard the name.'

'In that case, Mr Fanshawe, I really do think that, at least
for the moment, we may consider ourselves correctly introduced.'

Mr Fanshawe was not one to dispute this satisfactory
outcome. He bowed, and Sophie curtsied, and then they both
laughed.

'I am excessively glad that that is so satisfactorily settled,'
said Mr Fanshawe, sounding relieved.

'So am I!' returned Sophie. 'It would have been exceedingly awkward otherwise. But you will promise to call upon
me in London, will not you—so that I may make all right.'

'It is all right now, Miss Neville.'

'Indeed it is not, Mr Fanshawe! Please, you must promise
me.' She looked up at him beseechingly.

It would have had to have been a far harder-hearted man
than Mr Fanshawe to have denied that appeal.

'I shall be delighted to wait upon you, Miss Neville.'

'I am so glad, Mr Fanshawe.'

'At your grandmother's, Lady Knight's, in Portland
Square.'

'Yes.'

'Lady Knight is your maternal grandmother, I collect?'

'Oh, no. She is my father's mother, but she has remarried.
She is now a widow once more.' Sophie looked up into Mr
Fanshawe's face in high good humour. 'You know, Mr
Fanshawe, I feared you might be too gallant, and make
things difficult for me.'

'I would never wish to make things difficult for you, Miss
Neville.'

His look flustered Sophie, and she said hastily, 'I think I

had better go and see about my room, Mr Fanshawe. I must be certain that it—it is one I can afford.'

'I am sure our good host will do his best for you.'

They walked back to the inn. In their talk they had moved a little way up the road.

'Miss Neville!' exclaimed Mr Fanshawe, suddenly stopping. 'I have been so stupid! I really can not think why my brain is working so slowly.'

'What is it, Mr Fanshawe?' Sophie sounded quite anxious.

'Oh, I have thought of something useful, so do not be alarmed, dear Miss Neville. It is nothing bad. No, it is merely that I have just remembered that I have a portmanteau full of my sister's clothes with me. I am taking them to London for her for the summer. She will be there for the Season, you know. If you will permit me to say so, you appear to be much of a size. As you have no luggage with you, I will have the portmanteau sent up to your room. I am sure you will find something in it which may be of use.'

'Oh, but I could not!'

'Hairbrushes, and nightgowns and—and—things. And my sister is considered a very fashionable young lady, so you need not fear that if you appear in one of her gowns, you would be dowdy.'

'Oh, it is not that!' gasped Sophie. 'I am sure Miss Fanshawe is quite at the height of fashion, but——'

'I shall not take no for an answer, Miss Neville,' said Mr Fanshawe, smiling down at her kindly. 'I positively will not take a refusal. Were my sister here, she would certainly insist, and as I am in charge of her clothes, I stand *vis-à-vis* them in *loco parentis*, so to speak, to dispose of as I will. And, therefore, I insist you take anything you might find useful in her box. I shall have it sent up to your room, but of course—well, I hope you will not disappoint me. And if it will make you feel any better, I promise I will buy my sister a new gown to thank her for her kindness.'

'I do not know what to say,' said Sophie laughing, and

shaking her head. 'But I am sure *I* would not like a strange young lady wearing *my* clothes.'

'Oh, my sister has the sweetest nature in the world!' Mr Fanshawe declared airily. 'She will be only too delighted to have helped a lady in distress.'

'I suppose you are right, sir,' agreed Sophie with a sigh. 'I fear I look a sad sight.'

'Oh, my dear Miss Neville! I meant no such thing! You look charming. Quite delightful.'

But Sophie was not deceived. She shook her head. 'I will go and see this room,' was her only answer as she smiled and went into the inn.

The innkeeper showed her up to a rather large and comfortable room, which he insisted was very cheap as it was at the side of the house. But Sophie could not believe this, and insisted on knowing its price before agreeing to take it. The man named such a low sum that she thought she must have misheard, but he assured her that it was correct, and as Sophie suddenly felt overwhelmed by fatigue, she was thankful to agree terms. Her tiredness, however, was somewhat dissipated by the arrival of a large black portmanteau with an earl's coronet on the top. Sophie pushed open the lid and peered inside.

The first items she saw were two bonnets clipped inside the lid. Sophie almost squealed with delight as she saw them. One was of satin straw trimmed with bows of green ribbon and little yellow posies; the other was of soft green pleated muslin adorned with cherry-coloured ribbons. Her first impulse was to take them out and try them on, but mindful of their unknown owner, she restrained herself and instead took out the dressing-case which was fitted into the top of the portmanteau. Opening it, she saw that it was furnished with brushes and bottles with what looked like gold tops, but none of them bore any crest or monogram. Sophie felt vaguely surprised at this, and picked up one of the hairbrushes. Looking at it closely she saw clearly that it had never been used. There was not one single mark upon the back, and the bristles looked pristine.

Sophie hesitated again, but then by chance she caught sight of herself in the cheval glass, and her horror at the picture she presented drove her into a frenzy of activity with the hairbrush, and she did not stop till her curls looked once more their normal glossy selves. Then she took out the washing cloths, and pouring some water into a basin she took off her dress, regarding it now with some distaste, and washed away the grime of the day.

Returning to the portmanteau, she looked inside again. On top lay a cambric chemise covered with much delicate embroidery. Sophie took it out and held it against her. It looked quite new, and was exactly the right length. Underneath lay a pair of white silk stockings, and some green satin flats. All these Sophie tried on, discarding her own worn ones with pleasure. Next there was a dress of pale green muslin, trimmed with darker green bows. This too, she held against her. It certainly looked the right size. Carefully she slipped it on, tied the bands, and did up the buttons, and surveyed herself once more. Really, had she chosen the dress herself, it could not become her better. It might have been made for her so well did it fit.

The only thing needed to complete her toilette was a ribbon or comb for her hair. Sophie went back to the dressing-tray to see if she could find a pin or a comb there. For the first time she noticed that the bottles did not seem to fit their compartments. Perhaps, she thought, Miss Fanshawe has fitted up an old dressing-case. After all, there was that coronet on the portmanteau lid. In one of the little glass boxes she found some pins edged with brilliants, and she tried the effect of these. It was as she was looking at the effect these made that she suddenly realised that she was famished.

She stood undecided a moment as to how she should proceed. She had better count her remaining money before proceeding downstairs.

It was while she was engaged in this that there was a knock on the door, and in response to Sophie's answer, a maid entered bearing a laden tray. With a little bob, she spread a white cloth on the table in the window and set out the food.

'Master's compliments, miss, and he hopes this will be to your satisfaction.'

'It looks very well,' said Sophie, eyeing the food appreciatively.

'Just say, please, if there is anything else you need, miss.'

'No, no. I am sure this will be excellent.'

As soon as the girl was gone, Sophie fell on the food as if she had not eaten all day. This was far, far better than the coarse bread and cheese she had shared at noon with Jack Bean. In no time at all every dish was empty, and Sophie sat back and sighed with satisfaction. Really, she was managing very well after all.

She had intended descending to the public rooms in the hope of seeing Mr Fanshawe, but when she next opened her eyes it was quite dark. She could see stars winking very high in the sky, and she realised she must have been asleep for some hours. There was nothing for it but to go properly to bed and this she did, fumbling in the dark with the fastenings of the unaccustomed dress and groping for her own chemise in which to sleep. But sleep did not come again, and when dawn came at last, it was a tired and wan Sophie who rose and washed and put on her old dress.

Carefully she repacked Miss Fanshawe's belongings in the portmanteau, and idly wondered about the crest as she closed the lid. Then she descended to the eating-room and obtained a cup of chocolate and a roll. She knew that Jack Bean would be ready to leave soon, and feeling only slightly refreshed by the food, she sought out the innkeeper to pay what she owed. But to her astonishment, the innkeeper told her that all was settled.

'Your cousin paid all last night, miss.'

'My cousin!'

'Yes, miss.'

Of course, her mysterious cousin could only be one person, and Sophie felt too tired to argue now.

'I see. Well, will you please tell my cousin when he comes down, that the portmanteau is ready in my room, and please thank him for it.'

'Very well, miss.'

'I must leave now, but will you please tell my cousin that I expect to see him in Portland Square?'

'Certainly, miss.'

Luckily Sophie was not aware of the man's knowing look as she made her way outside to the cart. She would have been a great deal more uncomfortable had she noticed it.

The cart had not travelled a great many miles in the two hours since it had left the inn when a plain curricle, drawn by two good, but by no means outstanding horses, drew up beside it.

'Good morning, Miss Neville.'

Sophie looked up quickly.

'Oh, good morning, Mr Fanshawe.' For the first time that day, a little animation lit her features. Mr Fanshawe, seated beside his groom, was the best sight she could have had.

'We have another fine day before us.'

'Are you travelling far, sir?'

'No; I think it very unlikely.' He looked amused as he smiled down at Sophie sitting beside the carter.

'We do not travel far, either.' Sophie spread her hands a little to indicate her conveyance. 'And I must thank you, sir, for your kindness to me yesterday evening.'

'I hope the dinner was to your liking?'

'It was delicious. And I was so hungry! I had hoped to thank you afterwards, but—I am afraid—I fell asleep!' And Sophie looked rather rueful.

'Doubtless you were tired after sitting in the hot sun all day.'

'I expect that was it.'

They moved forwards without speaking for a few minutes.

'Would you care to ride beside me a little way, Miss Neville?' Mr Fanshawe ventured at last.

'That is very kind, sir, but—I do not think——' And to her annoyance, Sophie found herself blushing as red as her own hair.

'I thought it might make conversation a little easier,' Mr Fanshawe went on.

'You are right, sir. Perhaps——' Sophie went on tentatively after a little pause; 'Perhaps we might—walk a little behind the cart.'

'Are not your slippers too thin for that?'

'Oh, no, they are quite strong. And it is pleasant to have a little exercise. But perhaps you do not care for walking? I am sure Jack would not mind if we sat on the back of the cart.' She turned to the carter.

'That be quoite all roight, miss. Do'ee set 'ee there, and talk if you'm a moind to it.'

'I think that is an excellent plan,' said Mr Fanshawe with a smile. And handing the reins to his groom he jumped down from his curricle. The cart moved so slowly that Sophie was able to descend too without the cart stopping. They waited a little till the two vehicles had moved ahead.

'I fear you did not sleep well, Miss Neville,' Mr Fanshawe said in a concerned voice. 'Are you sure you wish to walk?'

'I am feeling better already, sir, I thank you. I trust all is safe in Miss Fanshawe's portmanteau. I hope she will not be very angry with you.'

'My sister is never angry. I told you she has a very cheerful temper: I assure you she will be only too pleased to have been able to lend you assistance. It is—unusual—to find a young lady travelling so—light.'

'Ill-equipped, you mean,' returned Sophie with a laugh, feeling better every moment. 'I only wish it could be said of me that I am never angry.'

'I am sure you are always quite charming, Miss Neville.'

Sophie shook her head. 'You are very kind, sir, but alas, it is not so. But then—as my cousin'—and here she darted a quick look into his face—'you will be aware of that already.'

Mr Fanshawe smiled guilelessly. 'I thought it might make things seem—more normal,' he said.

'I must thank you once again, Mr Fanshawe. But there was no need for such knight-errantry. I am not yet quite destitute.'

'Oh, Miss Neville, do not, I beg you, rob me of my noble deeds. There are so few opportunities for such in our modern life. And I have your grandmother's address in Portland Square. Lady Knight. Number twenty-three.'

'Number twenty-three! Is that the number?'

'Did not you tell me it was?' Mr Fanshawe said quickly.

'No, indeed, sir, for I did not remember it!'

'How very singular! Well, perhaps Lady Knight is some other number, and I merely imagined it was twenty-three,' said Mr Fanshawe easily.

At that moment a carriage which had been speedily approaching suddenly slowed down as it passed them. Sophie glanced at it and saw that it was drawn by a fine pair of chestnuts, and she noticed the groom before she looked away. He was the very same one she had seen with the earl's curricle on the two previous occasions. The man was driving the carriage, and beside him sat a young woman dressed very elegantly in pale blue.

With something of a shock, Sophie saw that the colour of the girl's hair was very like her own: a little darker, perhaps, but still distinctly red. The ringlets peeping out from under the bonnet were glossy and seemed to dance as the girl turned her head to watch them as she passed. The girl caught Sophie's eye, and her look of curiosity was immediately replaced by a broad smile. Sophie lifted her chin and gazed at the girl imperiously. Instead of turning away, the girl smiled more broadly than ever, and Sophie felt very annoyed. As if it were not bad enough to be trudging along in the road in a shabby dress! To be laughed at by this unknown female was more than flesh and blood could bear.

'Do you—do you know that young woman, Mr Fanshawe?' Sophie enquired furiously. 'She seems to be taking an unladylike interest in us.'

'Does she?' Mr Fanshawe asked blandly, looking up at the curricle for the first time. The girl now transferred her gaze to him, grinned more broadly than ever and appeared to give him a wink. Then she spoke to her groom, who whipped up the horses and the carriage dashed away. The girl turned round once more, her face laughing, and then she was out of sight round a bend. But before she had quite disappeared Sophie had time to notice the portmanteaux strapped to the back of the vehicle, and she saw again the earl's coronet painted on them. Well, if that female were indeed a Lady—a Countess—she should have better manners! Sophie was excessively shocked by the incident. She would ask Camilla about such behaviour when she saw her. She was quite sure that the young woman had *winked* at Mr Fanshawe!

'I had thought you might know her,' said Sophie. 'I have never known anyone stare so before. And I thought I saw you speak to that groom once.'

'Perhaps I did. Those chestnuts are exceedingly fine. One does not often see such a pair.' Mr Fanshawe spoke smoothly.

'Well, I am glad you do not know her, for I think she is a very forward female! I declare I have never seen the like!'

'Oh, very forward! Very forward indeed,' said Mr Fanshawe, doing his best to hide a smile.

'I am glad you agree with me,' pursued Sophie indignantly, not seeing his expression.

'Oh, some young women do not seem to consider it at all,' Mr Fanshawe went on. 'It really is exceedingly shocking.

The things some young females do nowadays—I can hardly refer to them as ladies—is past all belief!'

'Are the females in London Society often—so very—forward——' asked Sophie, her eyes round. 'I—I have heard my stepfather—well, I know he does not approve of all that goes on in Society, for I have heard him say so, but I had not thought it near so bad as this! Why! I am quite sure I saw her *winking* at you!'

'I am afraid that is very likely. Some females will stop at nothing!'

'You alarm me, Mr Fanshawe! My friend, Miss Camilla Hetherington, had told me that she had actually been presented to a Duchess wearing rouge, but I could not imagine anything worse than that!'

'But you ran away from home—to go in to this Society?'

'I had nowhere else to go. And I could not marry a bald man.'

'Bald!' Mr Fanshawe sounded much astonished. 'You have met—the—er—your proposed suitor, then? I thought you said——'

'Oh, no! I have not met him. But I am sure he is bald. I just feel it.'

'I see. And can you tell me anything else about him?'

'I collect that he is very rich.'

'Would not you like to marry a rich man?'

'Oh, yes! It would be very agreeable. My stepfather is not so very rich, you see, and it would be best if I could settle down comfortably. I quite see that. But I do not want to marry an old man just for that. I hope to meet—someone more agreeable—when I come out.'

'You are not yet out, then?'

'No.' Sophie could not help her blush. 'I—I am afraid you will think me as bad as the young woman of whom we have just been speaking.'

'Oh no! For I quite understand that desperate circumstances require desperate measures. And I am certain you will find someone very agreeable—who is also rich—when you do come out. London Society is not all bad, I assure you. I know a great many very pleasant young gentlemen.'

'I am sure there must be many of them. In all one reads about London Society, there always seem to be a number of exceptionally delightful people.'

'Ah, Miss Neville, you keep up with the gossip columns, I see!'

'Oh no, sir! For I am not really allowed to see them. I do not manage it very often. No, I was referring to books.'

'I see,' he said, giving her a quizzical smile.

'Do not you think, perhaps, Mr Fanshawe, we should catch up with our carriages?' Sophie said, noticing suddenly how far behind they were. 'They are almost out of sight.'

'Oh! So they are! And you must be tired of walking, Miss Neville. I do beg your pardon. I have been very thoughtless!'

'Oh no, but you will wish to press forward, no doubt. And Miss Fanshawe will be waiting for her portmanteau.'

'No, I have all the time in the world. My sister is not yet in London. And I trust you have no objection to my escorting you?'

'Indeed not! It is most delightful!' And then Sophie blushed furiously.

'Then we are quite in agreement, Miss Neville,' he answered, smiling down at her.

CHAPTER
FOUR

To Sophie's delight Mr Fanshawe remained with her for the whole of that day, and during that time she attempted, in what she considered to be a most delicate and adroit manner, to find out as much about him as possible. But somehow, just as she thought she was on the verge of discovering something that would have been of very great interest, the conversation became diverted into another channel, and she was not able to return to the intriguing point.

But, assiduously, she did gather up every crumb of information about himself which he did let fall; at the end of the day she had to admit to herself that it was not so very much. He was a young man of some four and twenty years, of independent means, and shared a house in Berkshire with his sister. Although Sophie had not the courage to ask him directly, this item of information pleased her extraordinarily. Surely if he had had a wife, he would have mentioned her also?

She tried out in her own mind various phrases such as, 'And will your wife be accompanying Miss Fanshawe and yourself during the coming season?' but not once did an opportunity to make use of such a phrase occur.

However, nothing arose to disturb the satisfactory impression that Mr Fanshawe was not engaged in any way.

Sophie was entirely unaware that during the course of their journey to London she had, on the other hand, told Mr Fanshawe almost everything that there was to be known about herself. He positively encouraged her to talk, and Sophie had not the slightest objection to complying with his wishes, for he seemed to take a genuine interest in all that she told him.

She described her quiet existence in Mallowfield and how she was forced to rely, for practical guidance on Life, on the novels of the local circulating library. She explained how her stepfather, Mr Moreton, was always teasing her about the novels she spent so much time in devouring, and was much gratified to discover that Mr Fanshawe was not wholly unacquainted with the art-form; at least, he knew Mrs Radcliffe's story, *The Mysteries of Udolpho*, and listened with great attention while Sophie recounted to him the gist of the story in which she was then immersed, *The Prisoner of the Vampire*.

To her delight, her companion agreed with her entirely over the quite remarkable coincidences which there were between her own circumstances and those of the story's heroine. Sophie was particularly touched and in quite a glow when he expressed most sympathetic observations on the tribulations of being an orphan; and when it further appeared that he and his sister had lost their own mother barely three years ago, and he spoke most sensibly and movingly of their loss, she felt that there was a firm and unbreakable bond between them.

It was not long after this particular conversation when a tiny unfledged bird suddenly fell right at Sophie's feet as they were passing under some tall, dark trees that overhung the roadway.

'Oh, look!' Sophie had squealed. 'Oh, the poor thing!' And she had picked up the little creature and watched it compassionately as it lay palpitating in the palm of her hand. 'What can we do, Mr Fanshawe?' And she had looked at him anxiously.

'I am not sure that we can do anything, Miss Neville,' he had answered. 'It is such a very young bird.'

'Could not we find a worm for it?'

'We could try.' And Mr Fanshawe picked up a piece of stick and poked the bank at the side of the road.

When he did find a small worm and dangled it in front of the bird, the little creature took no notice.

'Do you suppose it will only eat flies?' Sophie cried. 'Oh, how I wish I knew more about nature! I should have paid more attention when my governesses tried to instruct me! But I confess, I was never much interested.'

Mr Fanshawe made a sudden grab at a gnat, but the little bird took no more interest in it than it had in the worm.

'How came it to fall out of the nest, think you?' asked Sophie, watching it sadly. 'It could not have been trying to fly yet. Its feathers are not showing at all.'

'I think it was probably pushed out by a young cuckoo,' Mr Fanshawe replied.

'I did not know that cuckoos do that!' cried Sophie indignantly. 'How perfectly horrid! I shall never like a cuckoo again! Oh, look! Do you think that——?'

And she held out her hand to show Mr Fanshawe the little bird, whose palpitations were growing slower, and then suddenly stopped.

'Is it dead?' Sophie had whispered, huge tears welling up in her eyes.

'I am afraid it is, Miss Neville,' Mr Fanshawe had replied. 'The shock has been too much for it.'

Mr Fanshawe dug a hole in the earth bank and they buried the little bird before hurrying on again after their conveyances.

'I suppose you think me very foolish?' Sophie asked, wiping her eyes. 'As well as very ignorant.'

'Not at all, Miss Neville,' Mr Fanshawe answered very decidedly. 'I should, on the contrary, have been extremely surprised had you not been affected by the circumstance,' and he had turned to smile at her with an expression of such kindness and understanding that Sophie had been forced to turn away her head very quickly, for fear he should see her tears welling up anew.

And for some time after that Mr Fanshawe had taken all the burden of the conversation upon himself, entertaining her with light-hearted anecdotes of his acquaintances till Sophie was thoroughly restored to her former happy state.

That evening Mr Fanshawe arranged Sophie's room for her and had sent up the portmanteau of his sister's clothes and begged Sophie to use whatever she needed.

'But I am sure your sister will not thank me for wearing her dresses. Everything appears to be quite new!'

'They have been made for this season.'

'Then Miss Fanshawe will need them!'

'She may always have more made.'

And when Sophie inspected the condition of her dress, she was very thankful to be able to put on again the green one which she had tried on before. It was quite extraordinarily lucky how well it became her. She dined that night with Mr Fanshawe in the public eating-room, and when she appeared downstairs she was very gratified by the admiring look in his eyes. This did much to allay her scruples about wearing his sister's clothes.

When they were in public, Mr Fanshawe always addressed her as 'Cousin', but sometimes, when she caught him looking at her, there seemed to be an expression in his eyes that was not at all cousinly. Sophie could not quite decide whether it was the sort of expression which *ought* to be there, but there was no doubt at all that she was very contented to see it.

Mr Fanshawe behaved always as a perfect gentleman, and made their situation seem as little unusual as he could and Sophie was grateful for it. And whenever she felt any misgivings, she reminded herself of the terrible fate from which she was escaping. She would never even meet the odious Mr Netherbottom now! Surely he would not want to meet her when he found out how much time she had spent alone in the company of such a delightful, handsome, young, attractive man as Mr Fanshawe.

How delightful it was that Mr Fanshawe was so agreeable! She would ask her grandmother to invite him to her coming-out ball; it was the least she could do. He might not be a nobleman and have a coronet on his carriage, and his carriage might not be drawn by a pair of magnificent blood horses such as she supposed Mr Netherton's must be, as he was so *very* rich. But it was he who had made her escapade not only tolerable but enjoyable; it was he who had smoothed out all the difficulties for her, and she was sure she would never meet anyone she liked half as well as Mr Fanshawe. And if they could be presented to each other properly—well, Mr Fanshawe did seem to like her and perhaps in time, he—— Sophie blushed at her own thoughts, but she smiled too. It did not occur to her that she had not read anything of Leonore's adventures for a whole week now.

When it became plain that Mr Fanshawe intended to remain with her to the end of her journey, Sophie's cup of happiness was quite full. She could not but admit that she was probably irrevocably compromised by now, but she refused to acknowledge that her reputation was entirely lost and kept up what proprieties she could. It was this that accounted for her being so adamant on one point: it was not until they had actually reached London and Sophie had said goodbye to Jack Bean, the carter, and was left to find her own way to her grandmother's house in Portland Square, that she agreed at last to ride in Mr Fanshawe's carriage. After all, she told herself, it was a long way to walk, she did not know the way, and it would be much better to drive up to the front door than to arrive on foot. She had seen how unaccompanied young ladies might be accosted, and she had no wish to endure the disagreeable experience now.

So, very gratefully, if doubtfully, she accepted Mr Fanshawe's offer to drive her to Portland Square.

As they drew nearer, Sophie's misgivings about her reception grew.

'I am sure Lady Knight will be quite delighted to see you,' Mr Fanshawe told her reassuringly. 'I really do not see how she could possibly be anything else.'

'I wish *I* felt so certain, Mr Fanshawe. But—I have not seen my grandmother for so long. I know so little of her. Nothing, really, except that she is very much in Society.'

And when they eventually turned into the square, Sophie stifled a little scream and clutched her escort's arm dramatically.

'Oh, Mr Fanshawe, my stepfather's carriage is outside! Oh, I can not possibly face him. He has come to drag me back to Dorset, I know! Oh, whatever shall I do?'

'But, dear Miss Neville, you will have to meet him again at some time. You can not avoid him for ever.'

Sophie bit her lip. 'I know, I know. But I had not thought to see him again here! Oh, please drive round the square again, I beg you!' She looked at him appealingly. 'I must think what to do.'

Mr Fanshawe shook the reins and the horses moved forward again.

'You know, Miss Neville,' he remarked after a while, 'your stepfather, Mr Moreton, will doubtless have been exceedingly worried about you. I do not think he will be so very angry, you know. More—relieved, I should think.'

'But I have behaved very badly, have not I?' Sophie whispered. 'Oh, it is all the fault of my terrible temper! I should think first! But—he took me unawares! I was so very frightened.' She paused for a moment. 'No,' she said sadly, and her shoulders drooped and she looked very woebegone. 'Oh, Mr Fanshawe, that is not true at all, I am afraid. I was not frightened. I—I lost my temper!'

She looked as if she were about to burst into tears, and Mr Fanshawe put his hand comfortingly over hers.

'I am sure you will find he will not be angry with you now.'

'He is never angry with me,' said Sophie in a small voice. 'He is always very kind.'

They passed the carriage outside number twenty-three, and Sophie eyed it somewhat fearfully at first. Then she looked at it more carefully.

'Oh!' she cried, surprised. 'It does not belong to my stepfather after all! But it looks so very like—I was quite sure at first. But this one has a coronet upon the door, I see—one with strawberry leaves—and that can not be my stepfather.'

'No, that is hardly likely,' Mr Fanshawe agreed gravely.

But Sophie did not catch the little tone of amusement in his voice for to her own astonishment, she suddenly realised that she felt bitterly disappointed. She would have been comforted to think that Mr Morton would be inside this strange house, ready to greet her with his kindly smile. She was conscious of Mr Fanshawe gazing at her compassionately as she forced back her sudden tears. She could not speak for a moment, then she said in a whisper,

'Would you put me down here, please?'

'Here? But we are but half-way round.'

'I know. But I think I had better go alone, after all.' She saw the look of doubt on his face. 'I—I should feel easier, Mr Fanshawe,' she said in a low voice.

'Very well,' said Mr Fanshawe quietly, and he drew the horses to a halt. 'I will wait here to make sure you are received——'

'You are very kind, sir,' said Sophie gratefully. She found it difficult to look into his face now. 'I—I do not know how I can thank you—for everything. You have been—you have done——' Sophie stumbled over her words, and it was all that she could do not to cry. In the last few days she had become so used to Mr Fanshawe's constant presence, his constant help and companionship—now she suddenly realised that she was to be quite on her own among strangers, and—and——

Tears welled up into her eyes at the thought that she might never see Mr Fanshawe again. Oh, but she would! She would! He had promised that she might repay him. She would have to see him in order to do that. Her words fell out in a rush.

'I can never repay you for all your time and trouble, Mr Fanshawe, but—at least—the expense—you have promised me that—I should never feel easy again, otherwise. I have your promise that you will call upon me here, have not I?'

Mr Fanshawe bowed. 'I shall certainly come, Miss Neville.'

'As soon as possible.'

'As soon as I can, I promise.'

He helped her down from the carriage, and she gave him her hand for a moment. Then, with palpitating heart, Sophie walked along the pavement and climbed the steps to her grandmother's front door.

A footman answered her ring.

'I am Miss Neville. Is Lady Knight at home?'

The man's eyebrows rose in a way Sophie did not care for.

'I am Her Ladyship's granddaughter,' she added, with a toss of her head.

The man's eyes blinked as he looked at her uncertainly. 'Her Ladyship has given strict instructions that she is not at home to anyone.'

'I am just arrived from Dorset.'

The man stood aside.

'I will inform Her Ladyship of your arrival, miss.'

Sophie uttered a silent sigh of relief. If she had been refused admittance, what would she have done? She could hardly depend upon Mr Fanshawe for ever, however delightful such a prospect was. Before entering the house, she turned and gave a little wave to the figure on the other side of the square, still standing by the horses' heads. Then she entered the house, and was shown into a little anteroom; the servant disappeared, and Sophie was left to sit uncomfortably on the edge of a chair, wishing that she were safe home in Dorset. In a few moments the man returned with the message that Her Ladyship was inextricably engaged, and would Miss Neville care to wait?

'Care to wait!' What else could she do? Sophie answered affirmatively with as much nonchalance as she could muster, and was then left alone again. She had hoped, she realised, for something better than this; some show of affection, interest—after all these years. She sat wondering unhappily what sort of person her grandmother could be. Oh, she should never have come. She should have stayed in Mallowfield and met Mr Netherbrow: she could have found some way of avoiding marrying him. She had been far too impetuous—far too—stupid. The full awfulness of her situation came home to her at last.

She tried to summon up enough curiosity to view her surroundings with interest. The room was evidently furnished in the height of fashion with a quantity of small tables and chairs with the slenderest of legs. Sophie wiggled in her chair and the legs squeaked, and she wondered if they would crack under her. She heard movements in the hall, but no one came to disturb her seclusion and her natural impatience began to reassert itself. She walked to the window and peered out into the square; the leaves were still quite a fresh green and there were children playing on the grass. Sophie wished she could join them. Anything would be better than this terrible waiting.

The door opened behind her and Sophie turned quickly expecting a summons to her grandmother. Instead, she was confronted by a man of about thirty, she guessed, very fashionably dressed but with a face so puffed and florid, she found him positively repulsive. The smile died on her lips.

The man stared at her for a moment or two, then he said in a drawling voice, 'Who the devil are you?'

'I—I am Sophia Neville,' Sophie gasped, astonished at his mode of address.

The man continued to stare at her in silence for a few moments, his face a study in insolence.

'I think we *might* do something with you,' he said at length. 'You look strong and healthy.' He lounged a little closer, picked up his glass and stared at her again.

'Well, Miss Sophia Neville, where have you sprung from?'

'From Dorset, sir,' Sophie managed to utter.

'Dorset! That's a demmed long way.' He continued to look at her appraisingly with his grey, slug-like eyes. 'How did she find you?'

'F—find me?'

'Yes. How did she find you? Dem it, girl, you understand English, don't you?'

Sophie had never met such a person before. She gazed at him, appalled, but too unsure of herself to be angry.

'Well, you've certainly got some looks, though you'll have to be smartened up a lot,' the odious man went on. 'I'd have preferred a bit more liveliness, I must say.'

The man now came right up to Sophie and chucked her under the chin.

Sophie's mouth fell open a little at this impertinence. She was too astonished at first to react otherwise. For the first time in many days her mind turned to her erstwhile mentors. She wondered wildly how the Duchess would have dealt with such a situation. 'How dare you, sir!' But no; the Duchess would never have allowed such a situation to arise. The Duchess would have quelled the man with one imperious glance. And Leonore? She had never been confronted with such a dreadful person. At least, not dreadful in this way. The touch of the man's fingers seemed to remain on her flesh, fat and loathsome like the rest of him.

Suddenly Sophie came to herself. Her face flamed, her eyes flashed and she scowled furiously. She raised her right hand and gave the man a stinging blow across the cheek.

'How—how dare you, sir!' she blazed. 'I don't know who you are, but one thing is certain, and that is that you are no gentleman!'

'Little devil!' the man exclaimed rubbing his cheek. But his mouth smiled though his grey eyes looked hard. He moved a step nearer to Sophie.

'I begin to think we may get on very well, after all——' the man began, but got no further. Sophie had put out her hands on either side of her to feel for some weapon of defence. Her hands encountered nothing but the folds of the heavy silk curtains, and grabbing an armful of the material, she pulled hard, and sweeping the end upwards she managed to drape it over the man's head. Turning to the other curtain, she tugged still harder and the whole lot came down, engulfing the man and herself too. She fought herself free with furious energy, born of anger, and shouted at the man still struggling in the green silk cloth,

'If you come any nearer, I'll scream my head off,' she raged oblivious of the fact that the man could not have moved nearer if his life had depended upon it. 'Oh, how right my stepfather was!' she stormed. 'I should have listened to him! He always said that I should meet unsuitable people in my grandmother's house, but I never—never—expected anything as bad as this! Dorset may be a long way away from London, and the people there may be very unfashionable, but never do they behave as you have done! You—you— you—hog!'

She glared at the struggling figure, and it was all she could do to restrain herself from picking up a little figurine she saw on one of the tables and breaking it over the man's bobbing head. She had not heard the doorbell ring, or the servant's measured tread across the hall as he went to answer it. She did not hear the visitor enter the house or the door of the little anteroom open. But just as she was furiously trying to think up another suitable epithet for the curtain-swathed figure, a voice behind her said, 'Ah, Sophie my dear, you are making yourself at home, I see.'

Sophie whirled round and saw Mr Moreton standing in the doorway, smiling at her. For a moment she could not recognise him, but when he began again, 'I am so glad to see that your long journey has not tired you too——'

He got no further, for Sophie rushed to him, flung herself on his breast and burst into tears.

'Oh, sir! How thankful I am that you are come!' she sobbed.

He patted her shoulder and said soothingly, 'There, there, my dear, calm yourself. I will look after you.'

The figure by the window had succeeded in extricating itself from the folds of the curtain, and was brushing itself down with much coughing.

Mr Moreton watched the man over Sophie's shoulder and said in a pleasant, surprised voice, 'Ah, Knight, you have taken up house-furnishing, I see.'

The man answered crossly through his coughs, 'Oh, it's you, Moreton. Well, have a care, I warn you. That little virago pulled the whole lot down about my ears, and is quite as likely to crack a chair over your head, I warrant.'

'I collect that you have not been introduced,' Mr Moreton said smoothly. 'Sophie, my dear, may I present to you Sir Lionel Knight, who has inherited the title from his uncle, the late Sir William, your grandmother's late husband? Knight, may I present my stepdaughter, Miss Sophie Neville, Lady Knight's granddaughter?'

The man glared at Sophie, then pulled himself together and managed a curt bow. 'Why did not you say who you were, ma'am?' he demanded grumpily.

'But I did!' Sophie gasped indignantly.

Sir Lionel gave her a glance, then pushed his way past them and they heard him stamping across the hall. Mr Moreton closed the door.

'Is that—is that really my grandmother's nephew?' Sophie said amazed. 'He behaved like a—like a——'

'I am afraid he is, Sophie. He lives here with your grandmother.'

'Here! Oh!' Sophie shuddered. She looked up into Mr Moreton's face. 'Do you know what he did, sir? He—he—chucked me under the chin! And if I had not pulled the curtain about him, I—I do not know *what* he might have done!'

'That sounds very like him.'

'But—does he always do that?'

'With certain—females, yes, I am afraid he does.'

'You mean—you mean—he thought I was—*I* was—one of——' But she could get no further. She looked at Mr Moreton appalled. 'But he should have *seen*—I mean—I do not sound like—I do not look like——'

'I fancy your dress has seen better days, my dear, though the bonnet is quite charming.'

Sophie glanced down at her dress and wished she had worn the one belonging to Mr Fanshawe's sister. If she had known what her present wardrobe would lead to, she would have stifled her scruples. As it was, all she had used was the hat after the ruin of her own.

'I still think he should have known,' she pursued obstinately. 'You would not treat any woman like that, would you, sir?'

Mr Moreton looked suitably appalled at the thought.

'My dear Sophie, you know that I—well, I do not think you need worry about him any more, now that he knows who you are. But now, my dear,' he went on, leading her to a sofa and sitting down with her, 'tell me about your journey. I am thankful indeed you are arrived safe and sound. I greatly feared for you.'

'Oh, sir, I was very bad, was not I?' Sophie wailed. 'I promise never to put you to such trouble again. I know how you dislike coming to London—and I am so very sorry for all the worry you have had, and oh, sir! You do not know how glad I am to see you!' she ended, giving him a hug.

'And you do not know how glad I am to see you, my dear.'

'I—I promise I will never be as bad again.'

'There really was no need for running away like that, dear child,' Mr Moreton went on, smoothing the hair back from his stepdaughter's forehead. 'I should not dream of forcing you into any marriage you did not like.'

'Oh, I know! I know! I was very bad. And very stupid. But you know my terrible temper! Oh, can you ever forgive me?'

'Of course I can, Sophie.'

'There—there is something else,' Sophie stammered, wanting to get the worst over and not quite knowing how to frame her sentences.

'Something else?'

'Yes. I—I—I did not have enough money with me and——'

'I hope you have not gone hungry, my dear?' Mr Moreton's voice was concerned.

'Oh no! You see—I—I was helped by somebody, and I have promised that I will repay him when I arrived here——'

'*Him*, Sophie?'

Sophie reddened. 'Yes. It—it was a—a young man—a—a Mr Michael Fanshawe—and he had been staying with Lord Barton, and I know he is a friend of yours and I thought that you might have met him and so perhaps he could count as an acquaintance and so it did not seem so *very* bad, and I should certainly have gone hungry had it not been for Mr Fanshawe and I know you would not have liked that and I might even have had to sleep in a barn, and so I thought it very much better and—and you will repay him, will not you?' Sophie was breathless. 'Mr Fanshawe has promised to call here so that I may repay him.'

'Certainly I must repay this young man,' said Mr Moreton, eyeing her flushed and excited face with interest.

'And I am sure you will not mind about it when you know him for he is a gentleman—not like that odious Sir Lionel at all!—and I thought perhaps—I mean—I would like it very much—if—if he could be invited to my ball—I should like it so *very* much,' Sophie ended in a whisper.

'A gentleman, you say?'

'Oh, yes. He always behaved most correctly.'

'If he is a friend of Barton's, I am sure he would. He will wait upon you here, you say?'

'He promised to come as soon as possible.'

'I am very glad to hear it for I should certainly like to make his acquaintance. I will write to Barton directly and ask him about his young friend. But Sophie, do not, I beg you, make a habit of accepting help from any young man who may offer it. You may—you may end up with a Sir Lionel!'

She shuddered. 'Oh, do not say so, sir. I could not bear it. But then, I should not accept help from such a person. Mr Fanshawe is not at all like that. He is tall and very handsome—at least *I* think so—and so kind and amusing—and I must say that if all the men in London are like Sir Lionel, you were quite right not to want me to come here, but I assure you, Mr Fanshawe is not at all like that——'

'Oh, there are some very pleasant people in London. I have met several I like exceedingly.'

'Have you been in London long, then, sir?' asked Sophie, surprised.

'A day or so. A day or so,' said Mr Moreton evasively.

'I thought you had but just arrived.' Sophie looked puzzled. 'It is very strange then that you did not pass us upon the road.'

'I must have missed you somewhere along the way. I kept a sharp look-out for you, but when I did not see you I wondered if I had judged wrong, and you had departed for

Gretna Green after all. Though I admit it did puzzle me as to whom you might have accompanied there.'

'Oh sir, now you are laughing at me,' Sophie smiled ruefully.

'Not at all. My first reaction was to send the servants to scour the country looking for you. But on more reflection I thought you must be coming here to your grandmother. But you have not yet told me how you travelled here. Did you come all the way from Mallowfield with this Mr Fanshawe?'

'Oh no! I came up with Jack Bean, the carter. It was a sadly slow and tedious journey. *I* am but just arrived, you see. If it had not been for Mr Fanshawe I do not know how I would have supported it.'

'I am not surprised you found it tedious, travelling at that pace. But I confess I did not think to keep a look-out for *carts*, though daily I feared that you might have been murdered and that you would be found with your throat cut in some ditch.'

'Oh, sir!' squealed Sophie, 'do not say such a thing! You quite frighten me. Though I never once thought of such a thing upon the road.' Sophie caught sight of the heap of curtaining upon the floor. 'Do—do you think my grandmother will be very angry?' she whispered.

Mr Moreton's lips twitched, but he answered gravely enough.

'You *could* say it was an accident, I suppose.'

'But Sir Lionel—he will—oh, sir! He did look funny, did not he?' And Sophie could not repress a giggle.

'I have, I admit, seen him to better advantage.'

At that moment the door opened and Lady Knight sailed into the room, her auburn ringlets bobbing about her ears, a fashionable ruff about her neck and her figured silk skirt rustling delightfully. Sophie jumped to her feet and could not help staring. There was not a white hair or a wrinkle to be seen. Her figure was little fuller than Sophie's own, and she looked a great deal less than her admitted forty years.

Without being told, Sophie knew that this was her grand-mother, but a grandmother the like of which she had never imagined.

'Darling child!' the woman cried, holding out her arms to Sophie. 'Darling child, at last! At last!' And she laid her cheek against first one side of her face then the other. 'Let me look at you. Oh, yes,' she went on, holding her at arm's length with her heavily-jewelled fingers, hard as birds' toes, 'Oh yes! I can see you are my dear Henry's daughter. Not a sign of—a real Neville. You are just like him, my dear. Your colouring. Your eyes. But heavens, dearest child!' she cried, her face taking on an alarmed, not to say appalled look. 'What have you been doing to yourself?' She turned to Sophie's stepfather. 'Mr Moreton,' she said severely, 'how could you allow this?'

'Allow what, ma'am?' Oliver Moreton returned, a little alarmed in his turn.

'Her complexion, of course! My dear, what *have* you been doing to it? It looks as if you have been labouring in the hayfields! Never—*never* have I seen such ravages in one so young! You look at least *thirty*! And you are not yet out! Mr Moreton, you have not been looking after my grand-daughter at all, it seems. *This* is what comes of living in the country. Totally unsuitable. All genteel young girls should be brought up in the town. It is the only place. *This* sort of thing never happens in London! Let me see your hands!' she added, turning again to her granddaughter.

Sophie held them out. Lady Knight heaved a sigh of relief after she had inspected them. Then she closed her eyes and raised her face to the ceiling as if praying. 'Tomatoes—a parsley wash—cucumbers—thank heaven strawberries will be in soon——'

'I beg your pardon, ma'am?'

'I had feared worse. Much worse,' Lady Knight uttered in sepulchral tones. 'After what Lionel had said I feared the *worst*. But he has such very high standards. But this is what comes of letting a *man* have the rearing of a young girl. No sense at all for the really important things. But—by the Lord's grace and with Yvette's help—we will repair the ravages.'

She lowered her gaze and looked sharply at Sophie. 'And where *did* you have your clothes made? Do not you have *one* good dressmaker in Dorset? Really, I find it very distressing. I had not thought it of you, Mr Moreton; indeed I had not!'

Sophie looked down uncomfortably at her dress.

'It looked very well when it was new, ma'am,' she ventured, anxious to help Mr Moreton.

'And when was that?' demanded her grandmother. 'Oh, I can not think what Lady Ball next door will have thought if she saw you! She must have thought you the new kitchen-maid.'

'I am very sorry, ma'am,' Sophie began.

'It does not really signify,' her grandmother continued quite airily. 'Lady Ball is of no account. *Nouvelle riche,* you know. Her late husband made a great deal of money supplying arms to fight the Corsican monster, I collect. *That* is where the baronetcy came from. She is not at all the thing, of course, but she is so *very* rich, and she has such magnificent diamonds, one can not very well not receive her. Oh, and by the by,' she went on, 'what *have* you done to my dear Lionel? He interrupted my *tête-à-tête* with the dear Duke—which is a thing I never permit—but he came in with some extra-ordinary story about a country wench slapping his face, and pulling the curtains down about his ears, and he went off in a very bad temper. My dear, I must beg you not to repeat the performance. I am very fond of Lionel—he is like a son to me, and I am sorry you have got off to such a bad start, for I have some very interesting plans for you. But I hold you entirely to blame, Mr Moreton,' she added severely, turning to him. 'You have quite clearly not been doing your duty.'

And then, before Sophie fully realised what was happening, she was swept away, her clothes were removed and she was dressed in a bedgown. Lady Knight and her maid had a long conference and then her grandmother departed with injunctions to her to do exactly what she was told. Soon she found herself lying down with slices of cucumber laid all over her face and neck.

'And do not you move, miss. We can not 'ave you going into Society looking like that. I should be too ashamed. Why, in a good light, the mistress would look younger than you, and that would never do, would it?'

CHAPTER
FIVE

So there Sophie was.

And for a whole week Lady Knight and her redoubtable maid Yvette kept her more or less incommunicado: a sad change from the brilliant introduction to London that she had always imagined. And for once in her life, Sophie was rather in awe. After her initial confrontation with Sir Lionel, she seemed to have expended all her energies and was quite unable to find the wherewithal for even the tiniest tantrum. Which was just as well. For there was a very great deal to do, Yvette assured her, before Lady Knight, and more particularly Yvette herself, considered her fit for London society.

As Lady Knight so succinctly said, 'What would pass *in the country*, my love, would *never* pass here.'

Sophie submitted to the régime, dismally comparing her lot with that of Clementina in *The Cloistered Nun*.

True, she was given a daily airing, but escorted by Yvette, and only at an unfashionable morning hour, when nobody of note or interest would have considered appearing in public. She kept a sharp look-out for Mr Fanshawe, but the only other human beings who shared the Park with her at that time were nursemaids and their charges, and these could have no interest for Sophie.

The many fittings with the dressmaker and the shoe-maker and the modiste, she rather enjoyed. Having always been accustomed to a tiny allowance for such things, she was delighted to find that an astonishing number of exquisite and impractical articles were absolutely indispensable for a young lady's first launching upon the world. But unhappily, she had to endure other chores of a less pleasant nature, which Lady Knight and her accomplice insisted upon.

'Are you quite sure, my dear, that you did *not* help in the fields?' her grandmother asked several times. 'Really, I have never seen such a complexion—or lack of one—on such a young girl. Though to speak truth, to say that you have a great deal too much complexion would be a deal nearer the mark! What Mr Moreton can have been thinking of, I cannot imagine!'

And she left Sophie to the ministrations of her lieutenant.

Sophie found her face being bleached with parsley water to fade her freckles; she was washed in milk to soften her skin; her hands were rubbed with lemon juice to whiten them, and most horrid of all, she had poultices of squashed tomatoes laid upon her face to remove the havoc caused by the sun.

If ever Sophie was tempted to mutiny, Yvette had only to say, 'Na then, miss, I'll tell 'er ladyship as 'ow I can't possibly agree as you're nearly ready yet. It'll take me at least another week to get you right at this rate, and you knows very well that 'er ladyship'll never take you out without I gives the old say-so, so the sooner you gets this over the better it'll be for you,' for Sophie's grumblings to subside. Her eyes may have sparkled a little, but her tongue remained silent, and she would submit with a sigh to the next application of cucumber or marigold oil or honey.

Even her red curls were soused in egg and oil, and when she complained about the coolness of the rinsing water,

'It's freezing, Yvette,' she would wail, 'I can feel ice forming round my ears!' the only reply she received was, 'Na then, miss, you don't want to find bits o' *cooked* hegg in your 'air, do you?' and another icy cascade showered over her exposed head.

She had not even the solace of participating the while in the further trials and terrors of *The Prisoner of the Vampire*, for the biography of Leonore was missing, left, Sophie was certain, in Mr Fanshawe's carriage, and that gentleman, unhappily enough, had so far quite failed to put in an appearance.

Sophie felt utterly wretched, but tried to keep her spirits up. The first day in Portland Square she had been quite certain he would arrive, and each time the doorbell pealed she had been sure it must herald Mr Fanshawe. But to her severe disappointment he did not come, and it was only towards the evening that a short note arrived for her, begging her to excuse him and explaining that he had had to leave London unexpectedly upon family business.

Having read the missive once, Sophie read it again, and then several times more. Mr Fanshawe did not say how long he would be away from the capital, and with trembling lips Sophie determined to be patient. But as the days went by and there was still no sign of him, her resolution faltered, and she grew more and more despondent.

Clearly Mr Fanshawe had not grown at all attached to her after all, as she had hoped and thought.

She re-read the note a dozen times a day, treasuring it as the only tangible reminder of her acquaintance with Mr Fanshawe, and it was often all Yvette could do to get her out of the glooms by describing the many delightful encounters that awaited Sophie once she was 'out'.

When this treatment failed in its desired effect and Sophie remained sunk in misery, Yvette would alternate it with some brisk, business-like advice.

'Plenty of fish in the sea, miss,' she would say firmly.

'I know,' Sophie would sigh, 'but——'

'Never take the first pebble on the beach, miss!' Yvette would go on. 'You never know what you might be missin'!'

Sophie would give a wry smile at this and turn back to the matter in hand. 'Really, Yvette, to become an Accepted Beauty is an excessively tedious trouble!'

'You just wait, miss!' the maid would reply with a wink and a very knowing smile.

One morning, Yvette came in triumphantly bearing a plate of strawberries.

'*These* are what I've been waitin' for!' she exclaimed complacently. ''Er ladyship got 'is Grace to 'ave 'em sent up from Berkshire. The 'ole lot's to be used on you. The very first of the season, they is, and not one's for eatin', though to look at 'em it do seem a shame. Na, you put your wrapper on, miss, and I'll get some cut up.'

'Oh, let me try just one!' cried Sophie, eyeing the luscious fruit greedily. 'Strawberries are my passion!'

'Na, na, no stealin', miss!' reproved Yvette, slapping Sophie's outstretched hand. 'These are for your face, not your stomick!'

And before Sophie knew where she was, the delectable fruits were sliced up and laid over her own face and neck.

And after the strawberries had been allowed to work their miracle, Yvette looked at Sophie for the first time with real approval and actually summoned her mistress to inspect the new Sophie.

'Oh, yes!' cried Lady Knight delightedly after a close scrutiny. 'Now that really is a great deal more like it! I always knew there positively was *nothing* like a ripe strawberry. The dear Duke—*so* kind.' And she peered through her glass again.

'I really think I shall permit you to dine downstairs this evening, Sophie, my dear,' she went on. 'There will be only the dear Duke, of course, but I will ask Lady Ball to make up the table. She is always *so* glad to come. Afterwards I have a few friends coming in for cards—for the Duke, you know; he so loves them. And if this improvement continues, I shall be only too happy to take you to the Dales' ball next week! What do you think, Yvette?'

'I think we shall do very well, my lady,' the maid replied with a kindly, but rather complacent smile at Sophie.

'It is *quite* one of the events of the season,' Lady Knight added, 'and invitations are *much* sought after. They are called the handsomest couple in London, you know, though *she* has not quite enough *ésprit* for my taste. Such a surprise when Dale married the totally unknown Isabelle Harrowby—I remember poor Caro Barford's face—*so* put out. The ball is for his sister, the Lady Anne; such a dear girl! Though they do say she once—but never mind! Tonight you will sit between the dear Duke and Sir Lionel. I do not expect you to say much to His Grace, except to answer politely should he chance to address some remark to you. But I want you to make a point of being particularly pleasant with Sir Lionel. He is quite agog to meet you again, I assure you, and has forgotten all about your little contretemps. I want you and Lionel to become such friends. I have *great* plans for you!'

And with that Lady Knight floated out.

Sophie would have been all smiles and happiness at the news that at last she was to emerge into London society, even if it was only at such an undistinguished event as was proposed: a mere family dinner, she thought, a little piqued.

Her dreams had been quite otherwise. She had always imagined herself entering a glittering ballroom, arrayed in such a magnificent confection that every other female there was quite thrown into the shade. She would descend a broad staircase, and as she did so there would be a sudden hush, and then gasps would be heard as the full effect of her beauty made itself felt. Half-way down the steps she would pause and cast a regal gaze over the assembled throng. Then she would continue her descent to be met at the foot of the steps by a—prince—at least, who had hurried forward to claim her hand.

This—prince—of course, was, without any doubt, the handsomest, most fashionable, most desirable partner at the ball, and he had naturally been smitten by love for her at first sight. Now he singled her out before all as his future consort. This had been the delicious dream. The reality—well— perhaps it was not so bad after all: at least she would sit next to a Duke!

Yes, she was exceedingly glad to be coming out at last—but for one mote: she would have to meet Sir Lionel again. Sophie had not set eyes on him since he had quitted the room after their first interview, and the prospect of their second encounter she could not view with anything approaching equanimity.

She expressed her doubts to Mr Moreton when she saw him later in the day.

'I do not think you have any cause for disquiet, my dear. Sir Lionel is bound to behave correctly this evening—he is the host, and there will be other people present.'

'Oh lord, sir! Is that my only protection?'

'*I* shall quell any incipient boldness on Sir Lionel's part with a steely guardianish glance,' Mr Moreton said with a twinkle.

'I shall be very grateful for it, sir.'

'Sir Lionel is kindly looked upon in some quarters, I am told.'

'Well, I wish he were anywhere but here! It really does seem too bad! I had hoped, now that I am at last to make my come-out, that——' Sophie stopped abruptly.

'Yes?'

'It does not matter, sir.'

'If this Mr Fanshawe,' said Mr Moreton shrewdly, 'is as gentlemanly as you have told me, my dear,' and here he patted Sophie's hand kindly, 'he will certainly come to see you as soon as he is able. Something serious has, without doubt, intervened to prevent his calling here, you mark my words. His note did say "family business" I seem to recall.'

'Oh, do you really think that, sir?' cried Sophie, aglow again with hope. 'Oh, what a comfort you are! I am so glad you are here, though I am afraid it must be a sadly tedious time for you. I know you do not care for fashionable society, and I must own I was never more surprised than when my grandmother first told me that you had accompanied her to a ball.'

Mr Moreton looked at his stepdaughter rather wryly. 'Your grandmother is very persuasive,' he replied. 'And in any case, I am her guest and she will not let me escape. But—she does not make me dance, I am happy to say! I spend my time very comfortably playing cards with the Duke, who does not care for dancing either.'

'I am so glad you find His Grace congenial; I remember you were not used to approve of my grandmother and her friends.'

'I never thought your grandmother anything but a lady, Sophie,' Mr Moreton replied seriously. 'But I do think her choice of associates is somewhat—eccentric at times. However, I am thankful to have found that Lady Knight's standing in society has not suffered in any way—had it been otherwise, I should not have allowed you to stay here for long!'

'Oh, sir, I did not even know you *knew* about such things!'

'I have had to learn a great many unlikely things since I became responsible for you, my dear.'

'Really, sir!' Mr Moreton was constantly surprising her now.

'I have also had the pleasure of meeting my old friend Sir Llewellyn Godfrey again,' Mr Moreton went on with a quick glance at Sophie. 'He has been at several of the receptions I have attended with your grandmother. And quite apart from that my time has by no means been wasted, for the other evening I had the great good fortune to meet Dr Featherton from Oxford University—the one I missed at the Mallowfield Naturalists' Club, you know—and I have since spent two valuable mornings with him discussing his ideas on the classification of lepidoptera. When I return to Mallowfield, I shall be glad to rearrange my own collections in the light of his researches.'

'Well, I am very glad for that, sir. For I often feel guilty that I keep you from your work.'

'There is no need for that at all, my dear. I can well give it up for your season, and do so gladly. I want you to have a truly delightful time, and do everything that a young lady should.'

'And you are not the least little bit angry with me still—because of Mr Netherton, I mean?'

For a moment, Mr Moreton looked at Sophie with a very odd expression on his face. Then he said firmly, 'Not at all, my dear. I see now that it was an old-fashioned idea that would not do.'

'Oh, sir, you are so good!' And Sophie flung her arms round her stepfather.

Lady Knight came into the room at this point, fresh from her daily *tête-à-tête* with the Duke.

'And what do you think of your little haymaker now, Mr Moreton?' she cried triumphantly. 'Is not she much improved?'

'I had always thought Sophie very pretty, ma'am,' said Mr Moreton loyally.

Sophie stared at him in astonishment. He had never said as much to her.

'Oh, perhaps in a rustic way,' Lady Knight said dismissively; 'but now, surely you must see it, my dear sir, Sophie is very much more *comme il faut*.'

And so at last, Sophie made her come-out.

Before she went upstairs to dress for dinner, Mr Moreton had presented her with a small box which he bade her open when she was alone, and had looked at her with a loving smile.

'Well, Sophie, my dear, I know how much you have been looking forward to this day. Although I am, of course, still legally responsible for you until you come of age, or until your marriage if that should be sooner, I do not intend to be always overlooking you now, so do not think it. You are a grown woman and——' And here Mr Moreton surprisingly stopped, and there was a slight catch in his voice and a trace of moisture in his eye. 'And I am very proud of you,' he finished firmly.

'Oh, sir,' Sophie cried, much moved. 'Oh, sir, I pray that I shall always deserve your good opinion. You have been the best of fathers, for no real father could have looked after me more tenderly.' And she put her hands on Mr Moreton's shoulders and kissed him on both cheeks. She noticed again that he was beginning to look old; this time she observed it with compassion, and hoped that she was not responsible for all the lines and the grey hairs that she saw.

'Mind you,' said Mr Moreton in his normal tones, 'if I find you are proposing to elope to Gretna Green, for instance—with or without Mr Fanshawe—I shall certainly consider it my duty to post after you and bring you back by hook or by crook. I do not mean to be so lenient as that.'

Sophie smiled. 'I do not think you will have any worry on that score,' she said wistfully.

'Now, do not you worry about that,' Mr Moreton said briskly. 'All will turn out well, as I have told you before. Go and dress now. I look forward to seeing you in all your new finery.'

When Sophie opened the little box she found it contained a necklace of tiny diamond flowers on a gold chain, and a note from her stepfather.

'For my dear Sophie, on her coming-out day. From her loving guardian, Oliver Moreton.'

She noticed that the name in the lid of the box was that of the King's jeweller.

'Oh, sir!' she whispered, so moved that tears began to trickle down her cheeks. 'Oh, sir!'

She took out the necklace and held it round her neck. It was her first piece of real jewellery, and she immediately thought it the most beautiful necklace in the world.

When she went downstairs, having earned even Yvette's encomium that she 'looked a fair treat', she hoped that she might find Mr Moreton alone. She opened the door of the salon quietly and peeped in. She saw no one, so she slipped inside. It was only then that she became aware of a rather portly figure preening itself in front of one of the pier glasses.

Sophie let out a gasp. 'Oh!' She was startled, and the door slipped from her hand and shut with a bang.

Sir Lionel spun round.

'Oh, it's you, Miss Neville,' he said flatly and without a smile, after a moment spent surveying her. 'You're joining us tonight, then?'

'Yes, sir,' said Sophie advancing into the room, intending to put a good face on the unfortunate situation.

Sir Lionel did not seem as if he would add anything further, so Sophie went on, 'Lady Knight thought that I should make my come-out now.'

'Oh. Well, I must say that you look a damned sight better now, Miss Neville, than you did when we first met.'

Sophie gasped at this rudeness. The man was quite impossible! And she had been quite right when she had called him a hog that first time: he really did look quite like a pig, with his sharp eyes looking out of the folds of fat forming his cheeks.

'You are too kind, sir,' she said sarcastically.

Sir Lionel turned back to look at himself in the glass again. It was evident that he was highly satisfied with the set of his neckcloth for he patted it once or twice before he turned round again, looked Sophie impudently up and down, and said in a condescending manner,

'Well, I suppose you'll expect me to look after you, Miss Neville, as we are in a sense related—cousins of some sort I suppose it must be—but I must tell you that I run with a pretty fashionable crowd; I mean, they're used to rather more than country manners, and don't take kindly to new chits who know nothing trying it out with a real out-and-outer.'

Sophie stared at him, hardly able to believe her ears.

'And are all your friends like you, real out-and-outers?' she asked through clenched teeth.

'Oh, the very Pink of the Ton, Miss Neville, I assure you,' he went on in the same condescending voice. 'All, absolutely the Go among the Goes.'

'Well,' Sophie said, giving up any pretence at politeness, 'if their manners are comparable to your own, sir, I shall prefer to leave them to their—to their Cyprians and flash mollishers!' Sophie ended angrily. She had little idea what the precise definition was of the words she had used, but she had read them somewhere, and had concluded that they were somewhat derogatory terms for certain females.

For a moment Sir Lionel stared at her amazed, then he gave a shout of laughter which ended in his coughing loudly.

'By God, Miss Neville!' he spluttered, 'you'd make a pretty rainbow yourself!'

Again Sophie was unaware of the definition of the word, but she made a good guess at it. Eyes flashing, she advanced swiftly upon Sir Lionel and was about to implant a stinging slap on the cheek exposed towards her, when the door opened and Lady Knight's voice said,

'Well, here you two are! I am sure you have been getting along quite delightfully. Sir Lionel has been asking me all this week, Sophie, my dear, when I should permit you to appear; he has been in a positive fever of impatience to see you again, have not you, dearest boy? Now, Sophie, let me look at you. Ah, yes, Madame Odile has worked wonders for you with that dress; hold your shoulders back, child, you will ruin the line. Let me see your necklace, my dear.' Lady Knight peered at it for some moments. 'Ah, yes, *real* diamonds, but very small ones. I suppose they *are* suitable for a young girl. Now, where is the Duke?' she cried, turning from Sophie to the doorway, 'I had thought he was following me.'

At that moment a tall, elderly, pleasant-looking man

entered the room, followed by Mr Moreton. Sophie immediately ran over to her stepfather and kissed him.

'Thank you, sir! Thank you for my beautiful present. It is the best—the very best—I have ever had!' she whispered quickly.

'You look charmingly, my dear.'

'Come here, Sophie, dearest child, and let me present you to His Grace,' Lady Knight cooed.

Obediently, Sophie went to her grandmother who presented her to the Duke of Mayfair. She curtsied.

'I have heard a great deal about you, Miss Neville,' the Duke began, 'and have been looking forward to meeting you very much. Moreton has kept you far too long in the country.'

'You are very kind, sir,' said Sophie, dimpling up at him and seeing at once why Mr Moreton liked His Grace.

'Not at all, Miss Neville; it is always a privilege for an old man to be able to enter into conversation with a beautiful young woman; very invigorating, you know.'

The Duke was clearly about to say more, but His Grace's attention had been caught by something that was happening behind Sophie .

'Good God!' she heard him mutter under his breath.

Sophie turned to look too. A young woman had entered the room, not much older than she was herself, she judged. She had hair the colour of harvest corn, and was wearing the lowest-cut blue dress that Sophie had ever seen. She felt herself blushing even to look at the young woman. Sophie noticed that Lady Knight was staring in astonishment which quickly turned to outrage, but Sir Lionel had moved as quickly as his portly frame would allow. He bowed over the lady's hand.

'Oh, Sir Lionel,' she said in a heavily refined voice, from which traces of Cockney had not been completely eradicated; 'how delightful to see you again so soon.' She turned to Lady Knight. 'So kind of you, ma'am, to invite me to your little dinner-party this evening; I love small, intimate dinners of all things.' And she dropped Lady Knight a curtsy.

Lady Knight, strangely for her, Sophie thought, was still looking thunderstruck.

'I—I——'

'When I received your invitation, ma'am,' the creature continued, 'I said to Lady Ball, my mother-in-law, now isn't that the kindest thought! Here I have only met Lady Knight once, but now she has had the graciousness to invite me to an *intimate* family dinner. But then, you are such a friend of Lady Ball's, and she has always spoken of your good nature, and as you know, she does not go out much, so I do not see much company when I am with her. But I am only just out of mourning, and do not care for a crush yet, and a quiet little dinner is the sort of entertainment that appeals to me most.'

'Quite so,' Lady Knight replied grimly.

She proceeded to present Lady Ball to the others, but before there was time for more general conversation, dinner was announced, and the party proceeded downstairs. Lady Knight led the way with the Duke, and Mr Moreton moved swiftly forward and took Sophie's arm, leaving Lady Ball to follow with Sir Lionel.

'Who is she?' whispered Sophie. 'I thought my grand-mamma looked somewhat put out when she appeared. Surely she can not be the Lady Ball from the next-door house? I—I had imagined someone more—more my grandmother's age.'

'*That* Lady Ball is indeed older—but she is the dowager. *This* Lady Ball, or so I collect, is her daughter-in-law, recently widowed, I believe, and come to stay in Portland Square.'

'*Did* my grandmother invite her?'

'I should think it exceedingly unlikely. But somehow this Lady Ball has received your grandmother's card.'

Sophie looked at Mr Moreton with huge eyes.

'Sir Lionel seems to know her well enough. Do you suppose——?' and she gripped Mr Moreton's arm tightly and half giggled.

Mr Moreton vouchsafed no answer, but gave her a speaking glance.

CHAPTER
SIX

WHEN they were seated at the dining-table, Sophie found herself between Sir Lionel and the Duke and opposite Lady Ball. She tried hard not to stare at her, but found it very hard to take her eyes off the lady. Although she had never met such a person before, she seemed to know instinctively that, although Lady Ball's gown was obviously expensive, it was too low, much too over-trimmed and altogether in the worst possible taste. Indeed, the whole appearance of the female was one of vulgarity. Now that Sophie was closer, she saw that Lady Ball was a good deal older than she had first supposed: much nearer Sir Lionel's age in fact; she was clearly much helped by enamel, and her manners were a dreadful mixture of the excessively genteel and the girlish.

She and Sir Lionel had a good deal to say to each other, much of it in little more than whispers, and it was quite obvious that the two were on rather intimate terms. There was much giggling from her ladyship, and a good deal of patting her arm and offering her the choicest morsels from dishes on the part of Sir Lionel.

To Sophie he barely spoke. In fact, the sum total of his conversation with her amounted to no more than three sentences. The first was, 'D'you want some of this ragoo, Miss Neville?'

But he made no effort to help her.

His second conversational foray on Sophie's side was, 'Hopkins always does the turtle too salt: do you want to try it, Miss Neville?'

And his third, 'Floating islands again, I see! D'you have 'em much in the country, Miss Neville?'

With these three phrases, it was clear that he felt his duty to have been done, and he turned back with a simper to Lady Ball. That lady, once or twice, leant across the table to address Sophie.

'You are so lucky to live in the country, Miss Neville,' she said on one occasion, in her heavily refined voice. 'I quite dote upon the simple life; indeed, I am never happier than when I am in the country contemplating the manifold beauties of nature.' She laughed affectedly, and smiled at Sir Lionel. 'Such a pity you were not here for the *fête champêtre* that my mother-in-law, Lady Ball,' and here she glanced again at Sir Lionel, and a smile passed between them, 'gave a short time ago. It was a delightful start to the season, was not it, Sir Lionel? *Everyone* was there, my dear Miss Neville, simply *everyone*. But of course, Lady Ball, although now much retired, is so popular, and when she does give an entertainment, they almost fight for her cards. Is not that so, Sir Lionel?'

Sir Lionel agreed happily.

'Sir Lionel,' the lady went on, 'was so afraid I should be chilled by the damps, and would insist that I wore my cashmere shawl, but I was able to assure him that I am very hardy, though he affected not to believe me—the naughty man. It was just an excuse, was not it, Sir Lionel?' And she tapped the 'naughty man' on his wrist with her fan, and gazed at him archly.

Sir Lionel answered in an undertone and Sophie, feeling Mr Moreton's eyes upon her, glanced towards him. She could scarce restrain a laugh at his whimsical expression, and it was just as well that at that moment the Duke turned to address her, or her smile might have grown too broad.

'I really can not say how delighted I am to see you at last, Miss Neville. I had begun to fancy you were only a phantom.'

Sophie smiled. 'You are very kind, Your Grace. And it

really is entirely due to you that I am able to dine downstairs at last.'

The Duke looked surprised. 'Oh? How so?'

Sophie dimpled. 'The strawberries, sir,' she said in a low voice. 'It was exceedingly kind of you to send them, and I must thank you for them.'

'The strawberries?'

She nodded. 'Had it not been for them, Your Grace, I should be languishing alone upstairs still.'

'I do not understand you, my dear, but I hope the strawberries were to your liking.'

Sophie's eyes sparkled. 'Oh, I was not permitted to eat even one, Your Grace.'

'Not eat one! What can you mean? What did you do with them then?'

Sophie glanced at Lady Knight and saw that for the moment she was engrossed in conversation with Mr Moreton. She leaned towards the Duke.

'Lady Knight's maid cut them up and put them upon my face, sir,' she whispered.

''Pon my soul!' the Duke exclaimed.

'And they were so successful,' Sophie continued, 'that my grandmamma has allowed me to dine downstairs for the first time today. So you see how much I owe you, sir.'

The Duke leaned back to get a better look at Sophie.

'On your face, you say! What an extraordinary thing!'

'And very uncomfortable, sir!'

'So I should imagine. But I can hardly believe it was necessary to go to such lengths. Tell me, is it the usual practice with young ladies? In my day, strawberries were for eating.'

'I would much rather have eaten them, Your Grace. And it has not been only strawberries, I assure you. I have had a whole vegetable garden upon my face!'

'Good gracious!' The Duke's eyes twinkled. 'What caused all this—er—*cuisine extraordinaire?*'

'Lady Knight thought that I looked—totally unfit for the

polite world. You would never believe what I had to endure, Your Grace. Cucumbers, tomatoes, marigold petals, spermacetti wax, cream, honey—the honey was quite the most horrid. It melted on my face, you see, and ran down into my mouth. You would not believe how exceedingly unpleasant that was! And Yvette—that is Lady Knight's maid—she is an absolute dragon! I was allowed to escape nothing. Every day she devised something new and fiendish for me! *And* she slapped my hand for trying to eat one of your luscious strawberries. And all this because I had, perhaps, been in the sun a little too much. In fact,' Sophie breathed, 'Lady Knight said that I looked like a haymaker!'

The Duke looked suitably shocked, and Sophie was careful not to mention *why* she had been so exposed. She continued to regale her listener with a recital of the tortures she had been forced to endure, and the Duke listened, much entertained.

'I can see that you have indeed been exceedingly busy since you arrived in London,' he said seriously, but with twinkling eyes.

'Oh, yes, Your Grace!' said Sophie, nodding, so that her red curls danced round her face.

'You are determined to become the rage, I collect,' the Duke went on.

'It would indeed be very pleasant, sir, but to own the truth, I have no idea how to set about it.'

'I think you will do very well,' the Duke chuckled. 'A lively manner and a good dressmaker are more than half the battle. If you get yourself taken up by some influential Corinthian, you are sure to be made.'

'And how do I manage that, sir?'

The Duke laughed and patted her hand.

'You can wait for it to happen, my dear; I do not think you will have to "manage it".'

'But how shall I recognise a Corinthian, sir? Is Sir Lionel, for instance, one?'

'Good God, no!' the Duke blurted out. 'Oh, I beg your

pardon, ma'am, but—no. I collect that Lady Knight is to have a card-party later; doubtless there will be some there.'

'And will you point them out to me, please, sir?'

The Duke's eyes twinkled.

'I shall be delighted to do so—if it proves necessary.'

After dinner when the ladies left the gentlemen, Lady Knight excused herself for a moment, and Lady Ball immediately sat down close to Sophie and began to question her about Mallowfield; what size of property it was and how many horses were kept. Sophie would have liked to have given this dreadful female a good set-down, but as that was not possible, she answered as briefly as she could and made no attempt to contribute to the conversation otherwise.

But she had not to endure this catechism for long, for Lady Knight quickly rejoined them.

'Ah, Lady Ball, there you are,' she said blithely sailing into the room in the manner Sophie had come to know so well. 'I am indeed desolated that you have to leave us *so* early—it is such a pity—but I assure you, I *do* understand! I had not realised that you were but just out of mourning when I sent you my card, and that being so, you will not, of course, wish to undergo a crush just yet, and in any case you would not wish to offend the proprieties. I know how important they are to you.' And Lady Knight paused for the fraction of a moment to grace Lady Ball with her best hostess smile.

Lady Ball, who had at first looked startled, quickly recovered herself, and was now about to speak, but Lady Knight gave her no chance. She swept on,

'I know it is always so difficult when one becomes a widow—is it not, Lady Ball? Of course, I have had the experience on two occasions, so I know well that whereof I speak. It is a very uncomfortable situation because one always feels so *alone* in a multitude; there one is, surrounded by happy smiling people, all together, all with a—a *partner*, and one feels one's own loss suddenly with redoubled intensity. I would not for one moment, Lady Ball, subject you to such an ordeal, and you so young, so unprepared for sadness! Ah, Vickers,' she said as the butler appeared in the doorway, 'Lady Ball has to leave us now. See that she is escorted to her home. I must beg you to forgive me,' Lady Knight went on, turning back to Lady Ball who was still seated, 'if you have been caused any jot of embarrassment by coming here this evening. It was kind indeed of you to come so as not to put my table out, and I shall be ever grateful to you, but now we must not detain you longer.'

'There really is no need for me to——'

'I would not dream of asking you to stay longer, my dear Lady Ball,' Lady Knight's voice gushed forth anew. 'I simply could not do it. My conscience would not let me. So goodbye, my dear, and I beg you to give my regards to Lady Ball. I shall look to see her upon some other occasion.'

Lady Ball looked uncertain for a moment, and Vickers, standing by the door, cleared his throat impressively.

Lady Knight smiled down at her unwelcome visitor, her hand extended. If her face bore some semblance of goodwill, her rigid stance and haughty set of the head were filled with imperious command.

Lady Ball rose.

'Goodbye, dear Miss Neville, I have so enjoyed our little talk,' she said. 'I expect you will soon get used to our London ways. It must seem strange at first after no society to speak of in the country. I am sure we shall meet again soon; I will ask Lady Ball to send you a card for her next reception. She will be much pleased with you, I know; she can not abide what she calls "stuck-up" girls.' She smiled, but Sophie saw that her eyes were furious.

Lady Ball turned to her hostess.

'Goodbye, *dear* Lady Knight. I must thank you for the most delightful evening. I know that you always keep early hours. Lady Ball, my mother-in-law, always says that when one reaches the autumn of one's life, one must do everything

in one's power to preserve what little nature has left to one.'
Her eyes flicked superciliously to Lady Knight's auburn
curls. 'I do think you are so *wise*. Thank you once more.'

And she walked from the apartment with a toss of the head
that set her golden ringlets dancing. She was followed by
Vickers, who closed the door behind her with a final click.

Sophie wanted to laugh, in spite of the departed female's
impertinent condescension towards herself. She had admired
her grandmother's adroit turning-out of her uninvited guest,
but the lady had managed a good thrust home at last. Stifling
her mirth, Sophie peeped up at her grandmother.

'Odious creature!' Lady Knight snapped, her auburn
curls shaking with anger. 'I have given orders that she is
never to set foot across my threshold again.'

'But how did she come, ma'am? She must have received a
card from you!'

'Stole the one I sent to her mother-in-law, I have no doubt.
Or else it was all a plot between them! Odious, odious female!
I do not know how I endured seeing such a—such a *ladybird*
at my table!'

Sophie hid her smiles behind her fan and at that moment
the gentlemen entered the room. Sir Lionel immediately
looked about him, then demanded, 'Where is Lady Ball?'

'She has had to go home,' Lady Knight said smoothly, 'she
has the headache.'

Sir Lionel looked suspiciously at his step-aunt, then went
to lounge sulkily against the mantelshelf. Lady Knight
moved towards him and spoke in a low voice, but clearly with
some asperity. Sir Lionel scowled, but Lady Knight obviously persisted with her admonition, and glanced briefly in
Sophie's direction. After a moment's hesitation, he lounged
across the room towards her.

'Well, ma'am, and how are you liking London?' he asked,
flicking a speck of dust from his rust-coloured kerseymere
breeches with his cambric pocket-handkerchief.

'I have seen so little of it so far, sir, I can not tell.'

'Ah, well, that will soon be remedied, no doubt.'

Sir Lionel looked about the room.

'No doubt,' replied Sophie sweetly. 'And pray do not let me keep you, sir.'

She thought that Sir Lionel was about to move away, but he stayed and instead she heard him say 'Umm—er—hmm—er——'

Sophie looked in the direction Sir Lionel was looking and saw that Lady Knight was mouthing at him. She gave Sophie a dazzling smile and nodded as she noticed Sophie's glance. Sir Lionel turned back to Sophie.

'I wonder—er—if you would do me the honour, cousin, for so I suppose we must be—to drive out with me. I have the finest set of matched——'

'Cousin!' exclaimed Sophie, scarcely able to believe her ears.

'Er—yes. I believe that is how we must be connected. Lady Knight must make us some sort of cousins-in-law.'

'Never!' cried Sophie thoroughly outraged at the idea of being connected in any way with this odious man. 'Never!' she repeated more indignantly still.

'Oh well, there's no need to get into such a cut about it,' returned Sir Lionel huffily.

'No need to——' Sophie gasped. 'Sir Lionel,' she went on in a low, furious voice, 'ever since I entered this house you have treated me abominably! You have never shown me the slightest respect! I certainly do not now feel inclined to grant you the privilege of calling me "cousin" with all the intimacy that that would entail!'

Sir Lionel had now turned his head to give Sophie his complete attention for the first time. Gradually his expression turned to a leer.

'By jove, cousin!' he exclaimed. 'When you get in a dust you do look uncommonly fine!'

'How dare you, sir!' raged Sophie, jumping up. 'Oh, how dare you!'

Sir Lionel took a step backwards.

'No offence, ma'am,' he said hastily. 'No offence intended.'

Luckily they were somewhat apart from the others so their conversation had not been overheard. Now Sophie flounced down on to the sofa again and frowned at the rosettes on her shell-pink silk flats. Even though they were the prettiest slippers she had ever had, they were not now sufficient to distract her from the effrontery of Sir Lionel. Of all abominable creatures, Sir Lionel was the worst. No wonder Mr Moreton had wanted her to be betrothed before she came to her grandmother's house. He had wanted to protect her! She should have listened to him.

Her thoughts then naturally moved to the missing Mr Fanshawe. Perhaps he would come tomorrow! And now that she was out, she would be able to receive him without any worry that he might arrive at a time when Yvette had just put cucumber slices upon her face; and altogether, she thought hopefully, it was very well that he had not come yet. He would certainly see a great difference in her! He would be very much surprised.

'May I sit beside you, Miss Neville?'

Sophie looked up, startled for a moment, to see the Duke smiling kindly down at her.

'Oh, of course, Your Grace!' She moved to make more room.

'I collect that you have, as yet, seen very little of London,' the Duke said, seating himself.

'I have only been in the Park, sir.' She added with a rueful smile, 'In the mornings.'

'Ah! *That* would not be much fun. But things will improve quickly now, no doubt.'

The Duke looked towards the door as several of the after-dinner guests arrived.

'There are a great many very agreeable people here now, you know. That is the great pleasure of the London season, even for such an elderly creature as myself. Oh, yes, I am, my dear,' he went on in answer to Sophie's attempted protest. 'My dancing days are long gone, but I still thoroughly enjoy other, more sedentary, if not calmer pleasures. In the country one may find a handful of congenial companions, but one may have a long drive to reach them and they are not immediately to hand, so to speak. But during the London season, one may depend upon falling in with everyone one wishes to meet, merely by walking down a street to one's club. Oh, it is an exceedingly good system. The London season, you see, is not merely designed for the pleasures it gives to the young.'

Sophie acknowledged that she had not thought of it in quite that way before.

'I visit Bath as well, of course, in the winter. It is much the same there, with the addition that there one may persuade oneself one is enjoying oneself for one's health's sake. One glass of the vile water every morning is quite sufficient to put one in a good conceit with oneself for the rest of the day; one feels one has done one's duty. The rest of the day I spend in the way I like best.'

'I collect from Mr Moreton that you have a passion for cards, Your Grace?'

'One of the few left to me, my dear. Ah, how very lucky,' he said on seeing a tall, blond young man standing not far away. 'A Corinthian of the very first water. Henchley, my dear fellow,' he called, 'come over here and meet Lady Knight's granddaughter, Miss Neville.'

The Exquisite came over at once and dropped a graceful bow before Sophie. 'Your servant, ma'am.' The voice was languid, but the eyes were admiring.

And so Sophie made her first conquest in London society.

Lord Henchley was a thoroughly pleasant young man, who entertained her agreeably with his amusing chatter, and was her first partner when the company sat down to the main business of the evening.

Matters went on improving. Sophie found herself continu-

ally surrounded by three or four very polished young gentlemen, all of whom flattered her and paid her the most
extravagant compliments; and as she had never ever received
any before, she was delighted with them all, and was quite
unconcerned about any possible insincerity. This, she felt,
was what coming out was for.

The evening proceeded very pleasantly. Supper was taken
and Sophie, to her secret delight, found that there was some
competition to bring her refreshments. She accepted every
attention with aplomb. A return was made to the card-tables
and the group with Sophie was as intent on chatter and
laughter as the play. For the ladies' sakes, stakes were low, so
it was not unnatural that there was no very intent interest on
the outcome.

Because of the noise they were making, her group had
remained for some time unaware of a drama which was
taking place elsewhere in the room. But at last it was borne in
upon them that something rather out of the ordinary was
taking place.

'Oh look,' a certain Mr Lawrence said, glancing across the
room, 'there is something happening over there.'

The others at the table turned to look, and saw that
everyone else was gathered round a table watching persons
who were quite invisible to Sophie because of the press.

'Who is it? Can you see, Lawrence?' said Lord Henchley.

'No, but the play must be warm. Shall we go and watch?'

'Oh, do let's,' squealed a Miss LeStrade. 'I adore watching
high play; it gives me the most exquisite *frissons*.'

With one accord they all moved to the crowded table.
Sophie stood on tiptoe but could see nothing, so Lord
Henchley brought two chairs for them to stand on. He helped
Sophie up.

'Oh, it is Sir Lionel,' she said surprised. 'Who is the other
man? Do you know him?'

'He is called Thorley. Knight and he are a regular pair,'
Lord Henchley returned.

Sophie watched in silence for a few moments. Sir Lionel was sitting back in his chair, one kerseymere-clad leg crossed over the other. His cheeks looked a little pink, and Sophie concluded that that was due to the effects of the contents of the glass he was holding. From time to time he said a number. The other man was slightly older than his opponent. He had an upright military bearing and he was as lean and sinewy as Sir Lionel was plump. He held a pack of cards and every so often shuffled them, then turned one over. Sometimes a gasp would go up from one of the onlookers. To Sophie it seemed a very dull game.

'What are they doing?' she whispered at last to Lord Henchley.

'Knight is betting on the turn of the card.'

'It does not seem much fun.'

'It is if you make a monkey.'

'What is that?'

'Five hundred guineas.'

Sophie was so astonished she nearly fell off her chair, and had to grab Lord Henchley to steady herself. The man called Thorley glanced in her direction, and Sophie suddenly shivered as she saw his cold, hard eyes.

'You mean, each time Mr Thorley turns up a card——'

'Sir Henry,' whispered Lord Henchley.

'Each time Sir Henry turns up a card Sir Lionel may lose five hundred guineas?'

'Or win,' Lord Henchley replied with a smile.

'*Guineas?*' repeated Sophie, unable to believe it.

She turned back to look at the players. A new card was turned up, and there was a buzz of conversation from the onlookers. Sir Lionel took the pack and proceeded to shuffle the cards.

'What is happening now?' she demanded of her mentor.

'It is Knight's turn to deal.'

'Is that *all* that happens?'

Lord Henchley nodded, smiling.

'Well, I would much rather play at lottery-tickets!'

Sophie turned back to the players again. She really did not care if Sir Lionel lost five hundred guineas on the turn of a card—or five thousand. He was not only odious but stupid, and it would serve him right.

She looked at Sir Henry. He did not lounge back in his chair now that it was his turn to call, as had done Sir Lionel: he sat upright and his eyes never left the cards. Sophie would not have trusted Sir Lionel either. She certainly hoped Sir Henry would win. She glanced round the spectators; all were intent on the play. She noticed the Duke beside her grand-mother; they had eyes for nothing but what was happening on the green baize either.

This, Sophie sighed to herself, was not what she had come to London for. She wanted to drive in the Park, and dance the waltz at Almack's, and step through a quadrille at Carlton House, and see Mrs Siddons and Mr Kean, and gasp at the fireworks in Vauxhall Gardens—well, she knew it was now considered not at all the thing to visit the gardens, but even so—everyone admitted that the fireworks were very fine, and she would like to see them—then she wanted to go to the Italian Opera—and a masquerade at Covent Garden would be such fun—but she knew she would *never* be allowed to attend one. But it would be a great deal better than standing on a chair watching such a dull game as this.

She sighed again. If only Mr Fanshawe were here. *He* would not waste his time so, she was sure.

She felt someone's eyes upon her and turned her head to see Mr Moreton regarding her with one of his famous quizzi-cal looks. She smiled at him and shrugged. Suddenly she had a picture of herself as a child chasing round the grass at Mallowfield, trying to catch a butterfly for her stepfather. She smiled at him again. For the first time in a very long time she remembered that it had not always been dull in the country.

CHAPTER
SEVEN

IN spite of her somewhat disillusioning initial experience, Sophie went about her come-out with all the enthusiasm of her seventeen years. She went indefatigably to balls and parties and concerts and met quantities of delightful people, all intent on having pleasure like herself. Anxious to please, she was pleased, and Mr Moreton was much gratified by her success. Sophie seemed always to be polite and obliging now, and the only occasions on which she was likely to flare up were when Sir Lionel had been in conversation with her. She was careful to avoid him as much as possible, but this was not always easy, as Lady Knight continued to try to throw them together.

But Sophie had no need to depend upon the unwelcome attentions of Sir Lionel. She rapidly became very popular, but, in spite of what might have occurred, this did not turn her head. Being very honest, Sophie could not quite consider herself the rage of London. It was a vintage year, the connoisseurs said, and a great many very delectable young ladies were making their come-out, but she was certainly very happy with her situation. Driving in the Park, and waltzing at balls, were all that she had hoped they would be—though she had been somewhat disappointed when she had been strictly forbidden ever to mention the fireworks at Vauxhall again.

'Only servants and Cits go there now,' Lady Knight said firmly. 'It would do your consequence no good at all, and think of the people you would encounter there! No, Sophia, I do not wish to hear another word about it.'

When her grandmother called her Sophia, Sophie had learnt that it was better not to argue, for Lady Knight was quite capable of refusing to allow her to drive in the Park or attend a ball, and Sophie wished to miss nothing.

So Sophie went to all the correct places, and took an innocent delight in being sought after by such fashionable young men as Lord Henchley, and Sir Penistone Carver and the dangerous Lord Buckland who, Sophie discovered, had the most shocking reputation, and who had once offered to take her to see the fireworks at Vauxhall when she had mentioned them. She had been secretly tempted, but sedately refused, and Lord Buckland had laughed but did not press her. Apart from this one circumstance, Sophie was at a loss to account for his lordship's notoriety; he seemed in fact to be only lively—at least, he never presumed with her.

She was surprised and disappointed that she did not immediately meet Mr Fanshawe. The very first afternoon she drove in the Park at the fashionable hour she looked for him everywhere, and even when a smiling Lord Henchley rode up to her carriage and engaged in conversation, Sophie did not give her complete attention to her cavalier, but continued to look surreptitiously for the hoped-for figure. So great was her vigilance, in spite of the great press of carriages and riders and pedestrians, she was certain she could not have missed him had he been there. She wondered mournfully what family business it was that could possibly detain him so long.

At the theatre that evening, it was the same: there was positively no sign of Mr Fanshawe. She was tempted to ask some of the young ladies whom she encountered if they were acquainted with him, but her anxiety had suddenly rendered her strangely shy upon the point, and she was not able to bring herself to do it.

But if Mr Fanshawe was conspicuous by his absence, Sophie very quickly met her old childhood friend, Camilla Hetherington.

She had in fact sent Camilla a note the day after she arrived at Portland Square and had received a brief acknowledgement, but there had been no suggestion of a meeting in the reply Camilla had sent. Sophie had been rather piqued at this, but after some reflection put it down to the influence of Lady Hetherington. But because she had been rather hurt, she had made no further effort to meet her friend.

This particular evening, Sophie was attending a concert. She was not musical, and consequently was not much enjoying it, but it was a fashionable soirée, given by the Dowager Duchess of Milton, and her grandmother had insisted she attend.

'It would not do at all for you not to be there, child,' Lady Knight said firmly.

'But, ma'am, not only do I not care for music, but I can not understand Italian either!'

'That only shows that you should have attended to your governess; you have no one but yourself to blame. And it is quite beside the point. One has duties in society, Sophia, as well as pleasures, and I would not dream of offending my dear friend the Duchess by not bringing you. She is sponsoring the concert, you know, in aid of the St George Mission to Heathen Races. She has heard of you, and naturally expects to see you there. And please do not scowl like that or I will have to ask Yvette to put honey on those lines. And do stand straight, Sophie, or you will give yourself a hump!'

So, unwillingly, Sophie found herself at the concert. It was redeemed by the attentions paid to her by the Marquis of Buckland, and she passed the time during which there was the singing by speculating on how precisely he had acquired his reputation.

Now she was waiting during one of the intervals for Lord Buckland to bring her a glass of cordial when suddenly a well-known voice came to her ears.

'Sophie, deawest! I never expected to see you here!'

Startled, Sophie turned at the sound of the familiar voice.

'Camilla!'

They embraced delightedly.

'Oh, Sophie, I have been so hoping to see you. I wanted to wite and ask you to call upon me, but—well, you know what Mamma is! How long have you been out, Sophie? Are not you enjoying it? I weally did not expect to see you here this evening!'

'But Camilla, why not? My grandmamma tells me that everybody is here, but I assure you I did not want to come, but I was made to because the Duchess is a friend of my grandmamma,' Sophie laughed.

'A fwiend of the Duchess!' For a moment Camilla's eyes widened, then she looked at Sophie's gown. 'Oh, Sophie, your dwess! It is too divine. Who has made it for you?'

'It came from Madame Odile's.'

'Madame Odile's! But she is the most expen—oh, Sophie! How I envy you!'

'But your own gown is utterly charming, Camilla. I adore it!'

Sophie was ashamed of the little feeling of smugness she felt when she saw that Camilla's gown was, in fact, not near so fashionable as her own. In Dorset, Camilla had always had her dresses made by the leading Mallowfield maker, while Sophie had always had hers made at home by the sewing-woman. Then she would not really have been aware just why her present gown was so much better than her friend's, but now her eye was learning, and the difference was obvious.

Sophie embraced her friend again. 'Oh, Camilla, I am so happy to see you! I have been out but a few days; I suppose that is why we have not met before.'

'And how are you enjoying it, my love?' Camilla returned. 'I vow I have found it such fun. Such quantities of Cowinthians as one sees; I declare my head is constantly turning like a top to look at them all! Look over there—there is Lord

Dale—he is the Duchess's nephew of course—is not he the handsomest thing? But he is mawwied, you know. Then there is Lord Garstang. I see him in the Park evwy day: he is such a wattle! Then there is the Duke of Howden and that wicked Lord Buckland. They say that he is madly in love with Lady Dale, but she would not have him,' Camilla went on whispering behind her fan. 'Is not she the beautifullest cweature? Their ball on Thursday will be quite the smartest of the season.'

'So my grandmamma has told me. I shall look out for you there.'

'*You* are going, Sophie!'

'But of course,' Sophie returned, a little nettled at the amazement in her friend's voice.

But Camilla's face had fallen. 'Oh, how lucky you are, Sophie! Mamma has not received cards.'

'Not!' cried Sophie much amazed. By the way Lady Hetherington had been used to talk in Mallowfield, she had made sure that Camilla would be going to everything.

Camilla shook her head, but further conversation was cut short by the reappearance of Lord Buckland with the cordial. Sophie introduced him to her friend.

'I have not seen Miss Hetherington since she left Dorset, and that is an age ago.'

'And so undoubtedly you have a great deal to discuss. You must first compare notes on your dresses and bonnets, and then you have to dissect minutely all your acquaintance, and I know how unkind young ladies can be when engaged in that occupation.'

'For shame, sir,' cried Sophie laughing.

'I have experienced it too often,' Lord Buckland said mournfully, but with a gleam in his eyes.

'Well, in your case I expect it was deserved,' retorted Sophie with a smile, 'for I recollect you showed no very nice feelings the other evening when you were telling me such scandalous things about the other guests at Lady Davenport's ball. If you hear the truth about yourself on occasion, it will be only fair.'

'Ah, Miss Neville, you are too honest; I cannot bear it.'

Lord Buckland was about to say something more, but his attention was caught for a moment. Then he turned back to Sophie and Camilla.

'I beg your pardon, Miss Hetherington, Miss Neville, but I collect that my mother wishes me to go to her. If you would excuse me for a moment——?'

'Of course, my lord.'

'And please do not tear me completely to rags when I am gone.'

'We have other topics to discuss,' reproved Sophie severely.

'*Dear* Miss Neville; I shall not be long.'

When he had gone, Camilla looked at Sophie with round eyes.

'Sophie!' she breathed. 'Lord Buckland! He is the biggest wake in London, I am told! How come you to know him so well?'

'Oh, I know he is considered *dangerous*,' Sophie said nonchalantly, 'but I met him at my grandmamma's, and he has always been exceedingly *comme il faut* with me.'

'Your grandmamma, Lady Knight, is excessively fashionable, is not she,' sighed Camilla, a trifle soulfully. 'I can see that you have changed vewy much since you came to London. You look quite the thing!'

Sophie was just about to remonstrate with her friend when she saw Camilla's face suddenly brighten, a rosy hue suffused her cheeks and modestly she dropped a curtsy. She turned to see whom her friend was thus saluting, and saw a pleasant-looking young man with an engagingly open face bowing towards Camilla. Sophie turned back to Camilla and looked at her closely, noting her delighted smile with much interest.

'That young man is a—friend of yours, Camilla?'

Camilla nodded, still smiling.

'What is his name? I do not think I have seen him before.'

'He—he is a—a Mr Martin. His father is a clergy-man—and—and a perfect gentleman, you know.'

'I am sure he is,' Sophie cried, seeing that Camilla needed reassurance. 'Only——'

'Only what?' demanded Camilla, somewhat hotly.

'I was only going to say that I am sure any friend of yours must be such,' Sophie replied placatingly.

'Oh, I thought you were going to say that——' She stopped and looked confused.

'What is it, Camilla?' Sophie asked, now much interested.

'N—nothing.'

'Come, Camilla,' said Sophie, linking her arm through her friend's, 'you can tell me about Mr Martin. I will not tell a soul, I promise you.'

Camilla hesitated for a second, then she turned to Sophie, her face tragic.

'Oh, Sophie, I am so vewy unhappy! Mamma, you see, does not like my acquaintance with Mr Martin above half, but—but—he is quite the most delightful person I have met since I came out! He is so kind, and he never talks about things I do not understand—I know I am not vewy clever, but Mr Martin does not seem to mind that. But I am afwaid he is not at all wich, you see. As I have told you, his father is a clergyman and this Mr Martin is his *second* son, and so has no pwospects at all! And Mamma wishes me to mawwy Sir Henwy Thorley, but I do not care for him at all!'

And Camilla turned away and gave a little sniff.

'Oh, Camilla!' Sophie cried much concerned, 'you—you really have a *tendre* for Mr Martin?'

Camilla nodded without replying.

'And—and Mr Martin feels—feels the same?'

'He—he has never said so—in so many words, I mean. But I know he does. But *he* knows there is no point in speaking to Papa, for Mamma would never allow it, and in any case, whatever should we live on?'

'But—Sir Henry Thorley! I know him—or at least I met him the first evening I was out. He must be at least *forty*!'

'He—he is thirty-eight,' Camilla answered rather tearfully, 'but he is a vewy good *parti*, you see. And, as Mamma points out, I *should* be Lady Thorley.'

Sophie looked at her friend with compassion. It had been quite clear from her one glance at Mr Martin that he did not seem, however pleasant his countenance, at all well set up, and therefore he must naturally be a far from pleasing choice to Lady Hetherington.

'Where did you meet Mr Martin, Camilla?'

'At a party in Welbeck Street, shortly after we arrived here.'

'Welbeck Street? Where is that? I do not think I have heard of it.'

'It is somewhere near Cavendish Square—I think.'

'Well, that should be all right; I know I have already been to a party in Cavendish Square.'

'It—it is not the stweet Mamma objects to!'

'Oh, Camilla,' cried Sophie, thinking forlornly of Mr Fanshawe, 'what will you do?'

'I do not know, Sophie; weally I do not!'

At that moment they saw Lady Hetherington looking about her and moving in their direction.

'Do you wish to speak to Mr Martin, Camilla?' Sophie asked hurriedly. 'I collect you have not done so this evening.'

'Oh, Sophie, it is vewy distwessing! We are sitting so far fwom him, and we have not been able to exchange one word!'

'Well, you go and speak with him now; I can see him standing over there looking exceedingly unhappy. I will engage to keep Lady Hetherington in conversation for a few minutes.'

'Oh, Sophie! Mamma would be so cwoss!'

'She has not actually forbidden you to speak with him?'

'No; not actually *forbidden*——'

'Then do hurry, you goose! Your Mamma is nearly upon us!' And she practically pushed Camilla away.

She was staring innocently at the painted ceiling when Lady Hetherington reached her.

'Good evening, Sophie,' her ladyship said pleasantly. 'It will have been so agreeable for Camilla to have seen you again. I did see her with you just now, did not I?'

'Good evening, ma'am. Yes, we were able to exchange a few words. I thought Camilla looked charmingly.'

'Yes,' said Lady Hetherington complacently, 'she has had a very successful season so far. I have high hopes that before long we may have some surprisingly delightful news for you.'

'Oh, ma'am—you do not mean—surely you can not mean—but then you can only mean—is Camilla to be betrothed so soon?'

'Surely she mentioned it to you?'

'I had not collected that it was to be *soon*. May one know who the lucky gentleman is to be?' Sophie smiled up at Lady Hetherington with her most demure expression.

Lady Hetherington hesitated a moment. 'It is not to be made public, yet, so I suppose I should not tell even you, but as you are such an old friend of Camilla's—I hope to be able to put an announcement in the *Gazette* soon that Camilla is to be married to Sir Henry Thorley.'

'Sir Henry Thorley!' cried Sophie all astonishment. 'Not—not—*the* Sir Henry Thorley?'

'Is there more than one?'

'I do not know, ma'am. I have met but one.'

'*You* have met him!'

'He was a guest at my grandmother's house some days ago. There was a—a—a—card-party,' Sophie finished in a hurry.

'Card-party?' Lady Hetherington regarded Sophie with some surprise.

Sophie nodded, looked embarrassedly at Lady Hetherington, and then down at the floor.

'Sophie,' Lady Hetherington said urgently, then putting her hand on the girl's arm she drew her a little apart, 'Sophie, tell me about this card-party. W—What was Sir Henry playing?'

'I do not know, Lady Hetherington,' said Sophie all innocence. 'I did not play at his table. When I saw him, he was playing with Sir Lionel—five hundred guineas on the turn of a card, I was told, but it looked an excessively dull game.'

'Five hundred guineas!' Lady Hetherington fanned herself in some agitation.

'So Lord Henchley told me.'

Lady Hetherington opened her eyes wide.

'You have met Lord Henchley?'

'Oh, yes, ma'am.' Sophie smiled innocently. 'He and my lord Buckland are my most faithful escorts when I ride in the Park.'

'Lord *Buckland*! You know him also?'

'You called, ma'am?'

Suddenly Lord Buckland was beside them. He turned to Sophie.

'I do not think I have the honour of this lady's acquaintance, Miss Neville.'

'Oh, I am so sorry,' cried Sophie with affected surprise. 'I had quite thought you must be well known to each other. Lady Hetherington, may I present my lord of Buckland? This is Lady Hetherington, my friend Camilla's mamma.'

'Your servant, ma'am,' said Buckland bowing. 'I had the pleasure of meeting your charming daughter earlier.'

'You are very kind, sir,' Lady Hetherington responded, slightly confused. 'Sophie, my dear, I had no idea—I mean, it has been so pleasant to see you again. I hope we shall see you in Merriott Square very soon. I think the music is about to start again.'

'You are quite right, ma'am; and that is why I am come to

escort Miss Neville to her seat again. If you will excuse us?
We have to walk right to the front.'

And he steered Sophie away.

Sophie giggled.

'And what have you been up to, Miss Neville? No good, I
am sure of it.'

'On the contrary,' she said stoutly, 'I have done my friend
Camilla a very good turn.'

'Oh? How was that?'

'I enabled her to have some conversation—with—with-
—a—a friend.'

'Do I smell a plot? The lady's redoubtable mamma does
not approve of this friend, I take it?'

Sophie nodded with shining eyes. 'She wants Camilla to
marry—someone whom Camilla does not at all care for, and
who is twenty years older too!'

Buckland tut-tutted. 'That would never do.'

'Well, it would not,' cried Sophie defensively. 'Not when
she is in love with——'

'I knew I was right to leave you alone to talk.'

'I wish you had left me a moment or two longer with Lady
Hetherington!'

'*I* thought that lady looked somewhat put about.'

'She would have been even more so if I had had more
time!'

'Miss Neville—you are very wicked, I think!'

'Oh no, sir! But I have in the past undergone many slights
from Lady Hetherington——'

'And now you were settling the account!' Lord Buckland
finished for her with a smile.

'Not at all!' replied Sophie with great dignity. 'I was
just—hinting—to her ladyship that perhaps a certain
person—whom she *thinks* she would like for a son-in-law—is
not quite—well, might not be as suitable as she thinks,' she
amended. 'You see,' she went on, 'Lady Hetherington is
something of an Evangelical—at least, she always attends

Mr Fenton's church—he is at Hopewell, not far from Mallowfield—and he is a very rousing preacher—and so, she would not much care for a *gambler* for a son-in-law, would she?' And she turned her blue eyes on Lord Buckland.

'And,' said Lord Buckland, 'if I may be permitted to put what may possibly be an indelicate question—just how did my name come to appear in your conversation?'

'Oh,' laughed Sophie, 'I was merely enumerating the names of all the first Corinthians I have met. You would not have had me omit your name, my lord?'

'I will not have my name taken in vain——' began Lord Buckland.

'Ssssh!' admonished Sophie. The music is about to begin.'

When Mr Fanshawe continued to be so elusive, Sophie put all her dependence upon encountering him at the Dales' ball. On all sides she was told that the ball for the Lady Anne Fylde, Lord Dale's sister, was to be one of the greatest of the season, and surely he must appear at it if he was to appear anywhere during the season. At one or two balls Sophie thought she caught sight of the young woman with red ringlets who had so shockingly winked at Mr Fanshawe when they were on their way to London, and once she certainly saw her driving a very smart phaeton in the Park. But of Mr Fanshawe himself there was nothing. He did not put in an appearance at the Dales' ball, and afterwards Sophie decided sadly that she would never see him again and so would never be able to repay him. The latter consideration, she told herself angrily, was the important one, but provokingly her feelings kept telling her otherwise.

If he had been the least bit interested in her he would certainly have come to Portland Square before now. She had been quite mistaken in him, she thought furiously, and he did not deserve to have so much of her private thoughts. But she tried in vain to stop them. When she was in company, the nonsensical chatter of her partners kept her amused and she might even forget to look out for him for some time; as soon as she was alone, her thoughts immediately returned to him. She went over again and again every detail of the time they had spent together on the journey to London, and though it can not be said that in any way Sophie went into a decline, she did now seem to spend much of her spare time sighing and gazing soulfully out of windows.

Sadly she concluded that whatever impression she had gained when she was with him, Mr Fanshawe could not be in society; after all, everyone *in* society was in London at this time, and Mr Fanshawe was, quite simply, *not seen*. She remembered with a sigh that neither his horse nor his carriage had been of top class—but then, he *had* been the guest of Lord Barton, so that—but then, Lord Barton himself was not at all fashionable: he *never* came to London—and so——
It was all a very great shame, Sophie thought regretfully; she resigned herself to the melancholy fact, and flirted with Lord Henchley and Lord Buckland because of it.

CHAPTER
EIGHT

But Sophie was left little opportunity for moping alone. Ever since she had arrived in London, her grandmother Lady Knight had hinted that she had certain plans concerning her young guest and Sir Lionel. But Sir Lionel continued as odious as at first, and Sophie continued to avoid him as much as she could.

Now she suddenly became aware that she was very frequently left alone with him. At first she had always left the room as swiftly as she could, but in time this became inconvenient, and if Sir Lionel himself did not depart they would remain together without so much as one word passing between them.

One afternoon, as Sophie was driving with Lady Knight and Mr Moreton in the Park, they saw Sir Lionel's curricle dashing along as fast as the press would allow. Beside him was a woman with yellow hair and dressed in a most eye-catching green-and-white striped gown with a fringed parasol to match. The female turned her head just as the curricle passed them, and they were shocked to see Lady Ball smiling triumphantly at them.

Lady Knight remained stiff. But 'Odious female' was all she murmured to herself, then made no further reference to the incident.

At dinner that evening, however, much to Sophie's alarm, her grandmother remarked to Sir Lionel that Sophie had been very impressed by his equipage, and perhaps he could take her for a drive in the Park the very next day.

Sophie started to protest and Sir Lionel scowled, but Lady

Knight employed her usual tactics. She talked non-stop whenever she anticipated opposition to her wishes.

'It would be such a pleasure for her, Lionel, for you know that no one has a finer pair in London, and of course I could not permit Sophie to drive out with anyone but you, for you are so nearly related, and therefore the fact that you were seen together would not signify, and now that she is so very much improved since she came to London—the strawberries that the dear Duke sent were the turning-point of everything, you remember—I do not think you would need to be worried about what your friends might think. It is not too much to say, in fact, that Sophie would do you some credit, for she has had a most successful season, and Dale himself asked her to stand up with him at the ball for dear Lady Anne, and it was very much remarked upon, you know, and Henchley and Buckland have been very assiduous in their attentions, have not they, my dear? And I know I have seen Howden about and so many others that you would not be ashamed to know that I really feel you *should* allow Sophie to be seen with you, just so that you may point out to all these young Corinthians that you have the prior claim, and that she may naturally be more *intime* with you for it is really all in the family and that they are very much the outsiders and must therefore keep their distance——'

Lady Knight went on at considerable length. Sophie threw a pleading look at Mr Moreton, but even that gentleman was quite unable to insert a delay into the torrent of words. She hoped that Sir Lionel might flatly refuse to take her, but he did no such thing, much to Sophie's dismay and indeed astonishment. It was quite clear he had no liking for taking her into the Park, so why he should allow himself to be persuaded into doing so was beyond her comprehension. After all, Lady Knight was only his step-aunt. But persuaded Sir Lionel was, albeit ungraciously, and when all was arranged according to her satisfaction Lady Knight disappeared.

So the next afternoon, Sophie found herself seated beside Sir Lionel in his curricle, bowling along the streets to the Park. She had to admit that both the carriage and the horses were sufficiently impressive to attract a great many admiring glances, and Sophie was not at all adverse to these.

As they approached the Park gates, she glanced at Sir Lionel. They had not spoken a word since they had set off, and Sir Lionel's face was still set in sulky lines, and Sophie had no wish to have her new friends see her with such an ungracious cavalier. She took a deep breath and spoke placatingly.

'I know this whole outing is extremely disagreeable to you, sir, and I am very sorry that we were not able to evade it, but now that we are here, would not it be better if we both tried to put as good a face upon the situation as possible?'

Sir Lionel merely grunted, and swung into the Park gates so tight that he nearly brushed the pier with one wheel.

Sophie gripped the side of the curricle and held her breath. When they were on an even course once more, she made another appeal.

'One circuit only, Sir Lionel, will not take so very long. Let us make the best of that and then return to Portland Square.'

'I've been given my orders to be seen with you, madam,' Sir Lionel returned crossly, 'so seen we shall be.' And he went on scowling.

Sophie put a set smile on her face, and was thankful for the very first time that Mr Fanshawe did not appear to be in London. However fashionable in appearance was Sir Lionel's equipage, she felt she would have died of shame had Mr Fanshawe seen her with Sir Lionel.

At first Sir Lionel made no attempt to stop when he was hailed by acquaintances. He merely flourished his whip and drove on. Sophie kept her eyes straight forward, thereby hoping to avoid recognition by any of her friends and prayed for the ordeal to be over quickly. But suddenly the horses were brought to a sudden halt, and she had to grip the edge of the seat to prevent herself sliding to the floor.

'How now, Knight!' a loud voice called. 'You know Lady Ball, I think, but I am certainly not acquainted with Miss here. Won't you introduce us?'

Sophie turned her eyes to see a heavily-built red-faced man with a neckcloth so high round his neck that his nose appeared to be resting upon the top of it. Beside him sat Lady Ball, dressed completely in scarlet, her ensemble completed by a bonnet with a prodigiously tall crown, about which waved a sheaf of ostrich feathers of the same scarlet hue.

'My dear Miss Neville,' Lady Ball cried, 'how very delightful to see you again. I hope you will permit me to compliment you upon your gown, but then the first time I met you I saw that you had perfect taste: you always choose just *the* most suitable attire for a young girl. Sir Lionel,' she said, and gave the baronet the slightest of bows. She turned to her cavalier. 'Have not you met Miss Neville, my lord? She is fast becoming one of the rages of this season, and I made sure you must have met her upon many occasions. Miss Neville, may I present Lord Pimlico? He is a very old friend of mine.' She smiled brilliantly, then turned to Sir Lionel, her smile dimming immediately. 'Sir Lionel, I know you already know Lord Pimlico.' She stressed the 'Lord' ever so slightly.

'Devilish glad to meet you, ma'am,' said Lord Pimlico, taking off his hat and bowing. His eyes swept over Sophie then he turned to Knight with a grin. 'You certainly know how to pick 'em, Knight.' He turned to Lady Ball and took one of her hands in his. 'But I would not change *my* lady for all the blood-cattle at Newmarket. No offence, ma'am,' he said, leering at Sophie.

Sir Lionel looked decidedly put out.

'Shall I have the pleasure of seeing you at the masquerade tonight, ma'am?' he said to Lady Ball.

'Oh, no, Sir Lionel,' she said, simpering, 'I do not think so. Lord Pimlico has spoken of a reception the Lord Mayor is giving, and I think we have to attend that, do not we, my lord?'

'We certainly do, my—ma'am. Mustn't disappoint the City. You've been away from it for far too long, and we miss your elegance. You mustn't let us down.'

Lady Ball slipped her arm through Lord Pimlico's and smiled up at him.

'I think we should be on our way, do not you, my lord? I see there are many of our friends ahead, and it would not do not to greet them all. Goodbye, Miss Neville, I am delighted to have met you again. I have not forgotten that I am to ask Lady Ball to send you cards for her next reception.'

Lord Pimlico raised his hat again, and the other carriage moved forward. Sir Lionel remained still for a moment, looking sulky, then suddenly he whipped up his pair. They darted forward at once, and very luckily there were no other carriages to impede their hectic progress. Sophie hung on tightly, very alarmed.

'Sir Lionel, please let us go more slowly,' she gasped. 'There is not room enough for——'

Sir Lionel had been trying to turn his horses into a side path, the edges of which were lined with thick bushes. At the moment he was half-way across the main track, a phaeton, driven by a woman, dashed out of the side road and the hubs of the wheels of the two carriages became interlocked. The sudden jolt flung Sophie against the dasher, bruising her knees and one arm severely, and landing her ignominiously on the floor of the carriage. The tiger dashed forward to try to separate the two vehicles, and the lady's tiger did the same, but the united efforts of the diminutive attendants was insufficient for this.

Sir Lionel made no effort to help Sophie, but hauled on his plunging horses and glared at the occupant of the light phaeton.

'If you had but looked where you were going, madam,' he said furiously, 'this might have been avoided.'

'And if you had but driven more expertly, sir, keeping to your own side of the path, this would certainly have been avoided,' the lady retorted.

Sophie pulled herself off the floor, and seated herself again beside Sir Lionel. She rubbed her bruised arms and knees and picked up her parasol.

'Well, sir, and what do you propose to do about this?' the lady went on after some few moments, during which the tigers struggled again to lift one curricle wheel off the other. 'Are we to sit here all day? You will have noticed, I collect, that we are in the very middle of the path, and other carriages are unable to pass us?'

'If you had not been driving so fast, madam——' began Sir Lionel.

'Too fast!' the lady returned heatedly. 'If you had not tried to cut the corner, sir, if you had a carriage more suited to your abilities——'

The lady's voice stopped, and Sophie who had been looking ahead, trying to pretend that she was not involved in this altercation, turned to glance at her. Sir Lionel's face, she noticed, had grown from red to purple, and he seemed to be having difficulty in controlling his breath. But this was not what captured her attention. The lady driving the little phaeton was none other than the very same young woman with the auburn curls who had winked at Mr Fanshawe in so forward a fashion upon the London road.

Sophie had never felt so humiliated in her life. Of all the people with whom she might have been involved! It was so—so—degrading! Sophie wished that the ground might open to swallow them up, herself, curricle, Sir Lionel and all.

She stared haughtily into the far distance over the young woman's shoulder. The creature had the—effrontery—to stare straight at Sophie, with a broad, good-humoured smile upon her face.

The little tigers were continuing with their herculean struggles but still to no avail. Sophie became unhappily aware that a crowd was gathering, and that vehicles both before and behind were approaching to hem them in. There was a good deal of shouted advice from the bystanders and Sophie felt like cursing the ineffectual tigers as roundly as Sir Lionel himself was doing. It seemed to her that everybody in the whole Park had suddenly converged upon this small spot, and it was as much as she could do not to sink to the floor of the carriage with shame.

It did occur to her that she might simulate a swoon, but rejected the idea upon the consideration that Sir Lionel would be most unlikely to assist her, and her second situation might be worse than her first. But the horror was not to last much longer.

Two burly pedestrians now stepped forward and effected in a trice what the little tigers had been unable to accomplish. The red-faced but grinning tigers jumped up behind their respective carriages, and before Sophie rightly knew what was happening, to her immense relief the curricle moved forward again to a small cheer from the surrounding crowd.

She kept her eyes rigidly to the front, and miraculously a path seemed to clear before them, and Sir Lionel rounded the corner safely at last. But Sophie could not be unaware all this time that the young woman was still smiling in high good humour as she touched her own ponies to drive on.

Poor Sophie knew that she was scarlet with mortification. Of all the unfortunate things to happen! She should never have come out with Sir Lionel at all; the expedition was doomed from the start! It would have been better if she had flatly disobeyed her grandmother and refused to come out with this odious, incompetent boor! It was no comfort to her to reflect that she would never drive out with him again.

Neither spoke a word as they continued on their way. Each stared grimly ahead as if the other did not exist. The cross-path had brought them out near one of the gates to the Park. Sophie had thought that Sir Lionel would drive through it and return immediately to Portland Square, but instead he turned to make another circuit of the Park.

'I would prefer to go home, Sir Lionel,' said Sophie in a tight little voice.

The dreadful man took no notice.

'Sir Lionel, I wish to go home,' she repeated, louder this time.

There was till no response.

Sophie glared at the man who was still staring ahead, his eyes almost sunk in the folds of his face.

'Sir Lionel, will you please stop!' she cried furiously.

For answer, Sir Lionel merely flipped the reins insolently.

A wave of violent anger seized Sophie. On top of everything else that had happened, this was the outside of enough! She closed her parasol with a snap, and leaning across Sir Lionel, she grabbed the reins and hauled on them. The horses jerked to a stop and practically sat back on their haunches.

'What the devil do you think you are doing, madam?' Sir Lionel demanded loudly in a furious voice.

Sophie took no notice. Flinging down the reins she stood up and jumped down from the curricle and stalked off to the Park gate without looking back. She did not care if the tiger was staring after her with an impertinent grin on his face. It had been all she could do not to bring her parasol down about Sir Lionel's ears. *That* would have given his servant something to grin about!

She stormed along the street, oblivious of the stares of those she passed. Luckily she had left the Park on the Portland Square side and so did not have far to walk to her grandmother's house. She hurried along, panting partly from rage, and partly because of her speed of locomotion, and when she pulled the bell at number twenty-three, she nearly pulled the handle clean out of its hole.

The footman opened the door to her and she marched inside, not even bothering to reply to his greeting. She was

about to go up the stairs to her chamber, when Mr Moreton
came out of the small salon.

Sophie vaguely heard him speak, but not the actual words
he used. In a rush, she had crossed the hall and, flinging
herself upon him, had collapsed weeping upon his bosom.

CHAPTER
NINE

The whole story came tumbling out. Mr Moreton soothed Sophie and promised that he would never permit her again to go out with Sir Lionel. But even this, most solemnly promised, was not enough to calm the emotional Sophie.

'But—it will all be in the P—P—P—*Post* tomorrow!' she wailed, amid floods of fresh tears. 'Everyone I know will read of my disgrace!'

'Your disgrace! How were *you* disgraced?'

'I—I had to sit there—while Sir Lionel and that—that creature—shouted at each other!'

'I should like to have heard that,' Mr Moreton said in an interested voice.

'Oh, it was awful!' Sophie wailed anew.

'Come, come, my dear, I am quite sure there is no need for you to upset yourself so. Did not you find it—the least bit—amusing?'

'No I did not!' Sophie almost roared. 'There were dozens—hundreds—of people watching—and we held up the traffic both before and behind. It was the most embarrassing thing that has *ever* happened to me!'

'Did this other young person seem embarrassed?'

'No, she did not! She showed no nice sensibilities at all!'

'Do not you think she might have been embarrassed, but rather than show it, she pretended she was amused by it?'

'I do not know,' Sophie admitted doubtfully.

'She sounds to me,' said Mr Moreton definitely, 'the sort of person who would carry the whole thing off with a laugh. I can hardly think that *she* is talking about never showing her

face in public again! I warrant you, she will be driving in the
Park again tomorrow, and will dine out on the story of Sir
Lionel's discomfiture for the rest of the season.'

'But *I* was *with* Sir Lionel,' Sophie wailed again.

'But *not* responsible for his incompetence or inattention.
You had but just left Lady Ball, I think you said?'

Sophie nodded.

'And she was with some—some shocking Cit?'

'She called him Lord Pimlico.'

'Ummm. I fancy I have heard the name.'

'He was really quite dreadful, sir.'

'As bad as Sir Lionel?' Mr Moreton whispered.

'Quite as bad. Lady Ball has very strange taste.'

Sophie was getting over her snivels now. Her sniffs were
coming far more infrequently.

'Well, I shall speak to Lady Knight about Sir Lionel. I am
not having you upset again like this.'

'Thank you, sir.'

The next morning Lady Knight and Mr Moreton were
closeted together for some time in the small salon. Sophie was
in the morning-room, but could at first only hear the rise and
fall of their voices. She was astonished some time later to hear
her grandmother speaking in loud, angry tones. She peeped
out of the morning-room door and saw Lady Knight flounce
out of the salon. Her ladyship caught sight of Sophie and said
in a very cross voice, 'Mr Moreton is *the* most impossible
man! I simply can *not* conceive how you have managed to
support him all these years!'

Then in high dudgeon, with her auburn ringlets bouncing
about her ears, Lady Knight swept up the stairs to her
boudoir.

Sophie went to the salon and saw her stepfather standing
by the window, a frown creasing his brow. She went into the
room and closed the door.

'Whatever has happened, sir?' she whispered. 'My

grandmamma is in a high old pet and quite furious with you! What *have* you said to her?'

Mr Moreton smiled abstractedly. 'I am afraid there has been a—difference of opinion, my dear.'

'About me, I collect?'

'It is entirely due to—to a *quite* impossible idea that your grandmother has put to me.'

'Then it is certainly about me. What have I done wrong?'

'Her ladyship has made no criticism of you, my dear. I may say that had she done so, I should not have permitted her to proceed.' Mr Moreton's normally mild face took on quite fierce lines as he said this. 'But her ladyship realises that in this instance what happened was entirely Sir Lionel's fault. She has heard reports of the affair from other people, of course, as well as reading the account of it in the *Post*.'

'Oh! It is reported, then?' Sophie cried. 'What does it say?'

'It is here,' said Mr Moreton, handing Sophie a copy of the newspaper.

Eagerly, but with a trembling heart, Sophie read,

'There was an unfortunate encounter in the Park yesterday, we have it on good authority, when Miss F——'s phaeton was in collision with the curricle of Sir L——K——.

Both principals accused each other of incompetence in handling the ribbons, and it was left to two bystanders to part the entangled carriages while Miss F—— and Sir L——K—— proceeded with their argument. Sir L—— was accompanied at the time by the fiery beauty, Miss N—— who, we are informed, took no part in the fracas, but waited with becoming dignity till the carriages could proceed once more.'

'There, you see,' said Mr Moreton comfortably, 'you are mentioned in only the most complimentary terms. It is, of course, a great pity that you are mentioned at all, but that can not be helped.'

'A fiery beauty,' repeated Sophie, not at all certain that she ought to feel quite so flattered. 'I suppose that does not sound so very bad. But who is this Miss F——? I had thought she was a Count——' Sophie stopped in some confusion.

'Yes?' prompted Mr Moreton, watching Sophie's face carefully.

'I certainly saw an earl's coronet on her carriage, and I therefore thought she must be a Countess—she could be an earl's daughter, I suppose. But here she is called just Miss F——, so she is nobody after all, and—well, I am very much afraid that she is no better than she should be!'

Mr Moreton had a sudden attack of coughing, and Sophie had to pat him on the back.

'I—I do not think you should jump to conclusions,' he managed to say at last.

'You were going to tell me about my grandmamma's impossible idea,' Sophie said when Mr Moreton was restored.

'It really is of no consequence. I told her that it is out of the question.'

'Come, sir,' Sophie wheedled, 'it does concern me, I think you said.'

'It really is——' Mr Moreton began. Then he looked sharply at Sophie. 'I suppose I may be wrong about it,' he said with a sigh; 'perhaps I should inform you of it. Your grandmother put a proposal to me——' Mr Moreton stopped again, clearly rather ill at ease.

'Yes?' prompted Sophie.

'Lady Knight would like you and Sir Lionel to be married,' her stepfather said baldly.

'What!' cried Sophie, hardly able to believe her ears.

Mr Moreton nodded.

'What did you say?' she asked, with ominous quietness.

'I said I would never agree to the match.'

'Oh, sir!' And Sophie flung her arms round her stepfather. 'Oh, sir! The idea is too—too awful!'

'That is what I thought.'

'I hope you told her that I find Sir Lionel utterly odious!'

'Indeed I said no such thing! I made it quite clear that *I* would never agree to the match, and as I am your guardian, she would have to accept my decision. I put none of the blame—so to speak—on you. I do not wish you to quarrel with Lady Knight. No; it is much better that she blames me entirely.'

'But what can have put the idea into her head? She knows very well that Sir Lionel can not abide me, any more than I him. And he is for ever making sheep's eyes at Lady Ball—the young one! They are always together.'

'I know, my dear, and I rather think that it was Sir Lionel's obvious predeliction for Lady Ball that started this hare in your grandmother's mind. She does not at all want Lady Ball for her step niece-in-law.'

'I should think not indeed! She is most dreadfully common. But she and Sir Lionel *are* very well matched! And I collect that she is very rich. And I can certainly be of no interest to Sir Lionel in that way either.'

'I rather think Lady Knight intends to remedy somewhat that situation.'

'What can you mean, sir?'

'You must not forget that you are her only descendant. I am confident that she means to leave what Neville money remains to you.'

'Oh, I see!'

Sophie felt she had been very stupid, but that there was any Neville money had never occurred to her before.

The plans for Sophie's own ball went on apace. Lady Knight's cards were all sent, and a gratifying number of acceptances returned swiftly. The food was all decided upon, and the flowers for the decorations were to be sent up from Berkshire from the Duke of Mayfair's flower gardens. Most exciting of all, Sophie's ball gown was now ready and stretched out in the linen press, a dream of filmy silk chiffon of the palest green, embroidered with gold thread and sewn with pearls. Sophie was always taking a peep at it, just to reassure herself she had not imagined it.

A few days before her ball, Lady Knight summoned her

granddaughter to her in her boudoir. Up to this time, Lady
Knight had said nothing to Sophie herself of her wish for her
marriage to Sir Lionel, but when she received this summons,
Sophie felt the time must have come at last. She went to her
grandmother's room with a considerable amount of trepida-
tion.

'Do I collect correctly, Sophie,' Lady Knight began
pleasantly enough, 'that you are not attached to any particular suitor? You see a lot of Buckland, I know.'

'He is so amusing, ma'am; that is all. I also see Lord
Henchley a great deal, and several others.'

'I am glad to hear it. It does not do to seem too partial to
one particular person too early in your first season. About
now is the time for you to settle down and show more steadiness.'

'Steadiness, ma'am?' faltered Sophie.

'Certainly. You do not wish to gain the reputation of a
butterfly, do you?'

'Er—no, ma'am.'

'Of course you do not. No, as I say, *now* is exactly the right
time for you to begin thinking more seriously. As you are my
only grandchild, I have, of course, great plans for you. I
expect you know to what I am referring?' And Lady Knight
smiled a little airily at Sophie.

'Oh, no! Indeed not, ma'am.' Sophie said hastily, feeling
somewhat alarmed. 'Unless you think Lord Buckland wishes
to speak to Mr Moreton. But he has not said anything to me.'

'Buckland—that rake! Of course not, child; I do not mean
Buckland. No; I refer, of course, to Sir Lionel.'

'Sir Lionel!' gulped Sophie.

Lady Knight beamed. 'It would make me very happy to
see you two united in matrimony.'

'But ma'am,' Sophie said desperately, 'Sir Lionel is not at
all interested in me. In fact, he—he avoids me!'

'My dear Sophie, what *are* you saying? Why, only the other
day I heard him telling you about a visit to Brighton. He

would have liked you to accompany him, I know, but, of course, *I* was not able to leave London just then, or you might have had the pleasure of accompanying Sir Lionel to a ball at the palace there. Dear Lionel is such a crony of His Royal Highness.'

Sophie said nothing. The occasion Lady Knight referred to had been at dinner a few days before, when Sir Lionel had been recounting his version of a review of the troops at Brighton by the heir to the throne.

'Demmed pretty girls in Brighton!' had been his final comment.

If Sir Lionel had wanted to take a female with him, he would have been as likely to ask his step-aunt as herself, Sophie thought.

Lady Knight was looking keenly at Sophie. 'You know, dear child, that I have only you to whom I may leave the Neville money.'

Sophie blushed, remembering her conversation with Mr Moreton.

'I did not realise that there was any Neville money, ma'am. I—I had thought my father was quite a poor man.'

'Oh, do not say that, my dear!' Lady Knight held up her hands in horror. 'It sounds so—so—*mean*! But there is little enough, in all conscience. But what there is, I shall, of course, leave to you. Your grandfather would have wished it. The Knight money, of course, goes to Sir Lionel. I still have control of the larger portion of that, but eventually it must go to him. Now, my dear Sophie, it would please me greatly—it would make me very happy—to keep these two fortunes in the family.'

'I—I do not understand you, ma'am,' mumbled Sophie, looking at the pattern on the carpet, only too unhappily aware of what Lady Knight was driving at.

'Come, come, child! You are not so green as that! I want you and Sir Lionel to make a match of it!'

'But—but—Sir Lionel does not like me at all!' Sophie

cried. 'Why, when we first met, he even mistook me for a—a—ladybird!'

'Sophia! I do not care to hear you say such things!'

'But it is true, ma'am!'

'I am not referring to the fact, but to your choice of words. And I do not think you could blame dear Lionel for his mistake.' She regarded Sophie with some severity. 'You did look rather——' Lady Knight stopped on seeing the expression on her granddaughter's face.

'Yes, ma'am?' said Sophie with ominous politeness.

Lady Knight smiled brilliantly. 'What I mean, dearest child, is that you were hardly dressed *à la mode*. Lionel, as you have now come to learn, is accustomed to the very height of fashion in the females he meets in society.'

'Such as Lady Ball, I suppose!' Sophie muttered under her breath.

'Did you speak, dearest child?'

'Er, no, ma'am. But I had always thought,' she went on with mock ingenuousness, 'that Sir Lionel had a *tendre* for Lady Ball. The *young* Lady Ball, I mean.'

'That wretched woman! She is always running after the dear boy; she simply will *not* leave him alone! Oh, no, you may be sure that Sir Lionel does not give a jot for her, but she is anxious to get her nails into him. That is why it would be so much more comfortable for Sir Lionel if he were betrothed to some suitable person. And I have always dreamed of you two together—you would make such a fine pair!' She smiled sentimentally. 'Besides,' she continued, sitting up very straight, a grim expression on her face, 'can you imagine *me* being the dowager to Lady Ball?'

It was all Sophie could do to repress a smile at this, but she managed to return seriously enough, 'Er—no, ma'am!'

'So you see—it really is necessary for dear Lionel to be saved. And I should be delighted to see you following me as the next Lady Knight—as you have no particular attachment to any of the beaux you have met since you came out.'

Sophie's thoughts flitted sadly to Mr Fanshawe. Her grandmother spoke but the truth: she had already become attached to Mr Fanshawe long before she came out.

With an effort, she brought her mind back to the present. She realised that she had not heard her grandmother's latest words.

'I—I beg your pardon, ma'am. I did not quite catch——'

'I was saying that it would please me very much if you would put yourself out a little to be pleasant with Sir Lionel. He is very willing to be attracted to you, I know, and he is by no means an unacceptable *parti*. After all, I think you have no great hopes of a fine match among the swains of Mallowfield!'

Sophie was about to retort hotly, but gritted her teeth and answered as reasonably as she could manage, 'As you know, ma'am, until I am of age, I am completely under the domination of Mr Moreton. He can refuse to allow anything he does not like. Have you discussed your plans concerning me with him?'

Lady Knight looked at Sophie suspiciously at this, but made no reply, merely looking exceedingly annoyed. After a few moments' thought she said,

'You will remember what I have said, Sophie. I shall, *of course*, leave the Neville money to you, but—it is at my absolute disposal to leave as I choose.'

'Oh, yes, ma'am; I shall remember everything you have told me,' Sophie replied demurely.

She was thankful that Lady Knight had not thought to exact any promise from her.

From Sir Lionel's surly looks, Sophie suspected that her grandmother had also spoken to him, but that gentleman displayed no greater affability towards her than he had done before. Unnaturally often, it seemed to her, they found themselves left alone in a room together, but Sir Lionel never managed much conversation, and one or other of them always escaped as quickly as possible. She continued to find

Sir Lionel boorish and conceited, and often longed for former days when she might have enjoyed breaking a vase over his head. She regretted, indeed, that she had never done so while she had the taste for it, but she had grown more diplomatic now, she thought with a wry smile. And in any case, young ladies about to appear at their come-out ball should behave with a great deal more circumspection.

The final preparations for the ball were made, and at last the day itself dawned, fresh and clear: a perfect June morning. The ballroom was decked with white and yellow flowers, and the cooks had finished their assemblage of the turtles and the capon and the pigeon pies and the ox pallets and the tarts and the jellies and the blancmanges—enough to feed a whole regiment of the Iron Duke's army, Sophie thought as she gazed at it.

She surveyed everything with great satisfaction. All this was for *her* ball. This was to be *her* evening. For once there would be no doubt that it was *she* who was the rage of the town, just as the Lady Felicia Davenport had been at her ball, and the Lady Anne Fylde at hers, and Miss Fennell at hers. Sophie even succumbed with a goodwill to an extra application of honey and cream to her face by Yvette, so determined was she to leave nothing undone that would contribute to her success.

And when she was fastened into her ball gown and surveyed herself in the glass, she thought that everything she had been forced to endure had been worth while. Never had her skin looked so clear and translucent, or her freckles so invisible, or her curls so glossy and bright. She could not help smiling at her own reflection.

'What did I tell you, miss?' Yvette said with pardonable pride. 'You've got to *work* at things if you want to get them right. Not but what you *were* probably thought to be very pretty in the country—but in London, pretty girls are two a penny, and nobody gives them a second look. Your friend

Miss Camilla now, I could even turn *her* into a beauty if I got my hands on her, though to tell you the truth, miss, she'll never have your style.'

'I—I really am very grateful, Yvette, for all that you have done for me.'

'Bless you, miss, it was a pleasure. It's all up to you, now. You've got to make yourself a good marriage. Don't you go throwing yourself away on a nobody, mind. Promise me that!'

'I—I'll try, Yvette,' Sophie said, thinking nostalgically for a moment of Mr Fanshawe. 'I will try.'

It was with an innocent pride and modest consciousness that she was in her best looks that Sophie took her place beside her grandmother to welcome the first guests of the evening. There was only one mote to spoil her pleasure, and that was the knowledge that Mr Fanshawe would not be present. She had not been able even to mention him to Mr Moreton of late, so self-conscious about him she had become, but she told herself that he had now grown into a beautiful memory; she would never see him again, and while she was too young to mope for ever for what might have been, she would keep the memory of their days together as a very precious remembrance all her life: a beautiful, sad secret locked away in her heart.

She held out her hand to the first ball guest with a brilliant smile masking her wistful thoughts.

By now she had a very large acquaintance, and she found it very agreeable to be greeting so many familiar faces who were all part of the most fashionable section of London society. Lord Buckland arrived, as debonair and delightful as ever; he paid her his usual impossible compliments and made her promise him at least two dances.

'But not the first two!' she said gaily. 'I am opening the ball with my stepfather, Mr Moreton, and after that I am standing up with the Duke of Mayfair.'

Lord Buckland's eyebrows shot upwards. 'I do not believe

His Grace has danced these twenty years! You have made a great conquest there! I congratulate you. Will a mere Marquis do after such giddy heights?'

'If His Grace has not danced for so long, a mere Marquis who dances every day will doubtless be a great relief!'

And Sophie turned happily to greet the next guests. All her particular friends were there: Lord Henchley, Lady Felicia Davenport, Sir Peniston Carver, Miss Fennell—when Camilla arrived Sophie was conscious of a little feeling of shame that she no longer thought of her old friend in this select band; but the blame was hardly hers, she felt. Yes, all her friends were there, and many more: all filed past in turn and congratulated her upon the occasion, upon her dress, upon the brilliance of the company. Sophie was in a constant whirl of delight and excitement.

Now the ballroom was almost full and the guests were arriving more slowly. Sophie took advantage of a lull in the arrivals to look about her. The dancing must start soon, and she would be at the top of the first set. She felt impatient to begin. She turned to see if there were many more people ascending the great staircase.

A group of about eight had nearly reached the head of the stairs, and behind them Sophie thought she saw——! She shook her head in disbelief and looked again. Her heart gave a great leap and she stared, frightened her eyes were deceiving her. It was—yes, it really was—Mr Fanshawe! *Her* Mr Fanshawe. So he had come after all! Somehow he had received a card.

A wonderfully happy smile lit Sophie's features, and she was about to step forward to go to him, completely oblivious for a moment of why she was where she was, when the name of the first of the group was announced in stentorian tones and she was swiftly brought back to her duty.

She smiled at the newcomers as if they were her dearest friends; she was effusive in her greetings, thanking them *so* much for coming as if by so doing they were paying her the greatest compliment in the world. If the guests seemed surprised by her greeting they were too well-bred to show it, and Sophie was too happy to care. She would not look again: no, she would not look at Mr Fanshawe until he was actually before her and bending over her hand. She did not know how she managed not to jump up and down in her excitement. There! That was the last of the group before him: she had curtsied eight times. Now! *Now* he must be announced.

CHAPTER
TEN

'The Earl of Netherton and Miss Fanshawe,' the major-domo intoned.

Sophie turned her head sharply. Netherton? Netherton! But this was Mr Fanshawe—*her* Mr Fanshawe. She frowned as she saw him bending over her grandmother's hand. Then Sophie saw the female with him: it was the very same creature with the red curls who had winked at him when he was walking with Sophie on the road to London! The very same female who had been driving the little phaeton when she had been in Sir Lionel's curricle in the Park! So—the F had stood for Fanshawe!

The Earl of Netherton was straightening himself from bowing over Lady Knight's hand. Now he was moving towards her. He smiled at her: that same smile which made her heart turn to jelly in her breast and which she had been longing to see for so long. Automatically she held out her hand to him. There was no smile on her face now; it had been replaced by a look of utter bewilderment.

The Earl bowed over her hand, then looked into her face with laughing eyes.

'You are Mr Fanshawe?' Sophie whispered.

'The very same, Miss Neville,' he replied in the well-known accents.

'*And* Lord Netherton?'

'I am guilty, ma'am.'

'Oh!'

Sophie stared at him for a moment, remembering in a flash every little incident that had happened when they were together. *That* was why he had known the number of her grandmother's house though she knew positively she had never mentioned it. That was why——Oh, so many things were suddenly made plain! And Mr Moreton! Oh! How he had deceived her! He had known all along that Mr Fanshawe and Lord Netherton were one and the same! That is why he had not been at all perturbed when she had told him of her escort to London. He had known! He had always known! *Her* Mr Fanshawe to deceive her so!

How they must have laughed at her! How they must be laughing at her! How he must have enjoyed the joke as he accompanied her on her way to London! Making her believe he knew nothing of her; encouraging her to talk about the odious Mr Netherton—how he must have laughed then! Well, she had not been complimentary, she thought grimly, and serve him right! It was all monstrous! Monstrous! Well, let them laugh! Let them laugh! She would show him that she was not a female who could be so used with impunity!

'You are despicable, sir!' Sophie hissed through clenched teeth.

'Miss Neville—dear Miss Neville——'

With a glacial face Sophie turned from him to Miss Fanshawe and offered the tips of her fingers. The young lady was smiling gaily.

'I am so glad to meet you properly at last, Miss Neville. And I must apologise for our last encounter; I would not have had it happen for the world. When I saw it was you sitting beside Sir Lionel Knight, I knew that my guardian angel had gone to sleep for the day. And my brother was so angry with me, Miss Neville—you would not imagine! He even threatened to take my pony away and sell him when he heard of my escapade.'

Sophie bowed icily. 'I believe I have to thank you, ma'am, for——for—lending me certain items from your wardrobe. I hope their disappearance did not discommode you.'

'My dear Miss Neville, I was only too glad that my things

were there for you to use. It is always such a nuisance when one arrives anywhere with less than a full complement of portmanteaux.'

So! This—this Lord Netherton had told his sister about her discomfiture at the hotel! Sophie thought furiously. She glared from brother to sister. The creature was actually—*grinning*—at her, in a far too familiar fashion! Oh, yes, she could quite see that she had found the whole business a huge joke—and all at her expense! Well, if she thought she was going to be grateful to her for it, she would have to think again!

'It is such a relief to my brother to be able to appear in his right clothes at last, Miss Neville. He has had to be out of London a great deal, but when he has been in London, he has adopted a dozen different disguises to keep out of sight! I am very glad your ball has come at last so that he may be unveiled in all his new glory.'

'Indeed!' returned Sophie icily.

Some further guests now arrived, and Lord Netherton and his sister moved on. Automatically Sophie held out her hand and curtsied and smiled, but inside she felt a turmoil of rage and shame. To be so humiliated! It was quite unendurable!

'I did not know, my child, that you were acquainted with the Fanshawes,' she heard her grandmother saying with something approaching curiosity. 'He has but recently succeeded and has attended very few balls this season, though he is now considered to be quite the most eligible *parti* in society. It was quite different last season, of course. They say that his wealth is enormous now, though neither of those young Fanshawes had two pennies to rub together before this distant cousin died. Oh, yes, it has been an excellent thing for them, and *everybody* has been trying to catch him this year—you would not believe.

'I did not really think he would come this evening. I am afraid my dear friend the Duchess of Milton will be just the tiniest bit—*jalouse*—for he was not at the Dale ball, you know. Oh yes, Sophie, my dear, his presence here this evening is a very great feather in your cap!'

'Well, it is one I could well have spared!' Sophie muttered through gritted teeth.

'Do not you like him then, my love?'

'I—I hate him!' hissed Sophie, wanting to burst into tears.

The dancing started soon after that and Lord Netherton suddenly appeared at Sophie's side. She was delighted to be able to tell him that she was unable to afford him even one dance. No, positively not one. Every single one was booked long ago. She moved away on Mr Moreton's arm, still bubbling with rage and indignation.

'Oh, how could you, sir? How could you humiliate me so?' she whispered.

'My dear Sophie, such was not my intention. I had thought Lord Netherton exceptionally personable—indeed, I would even say handsome. But you positively refused to meet him, and as he was as positively determined to meet you, how could I prevent him?'

'But why did not you tell me that he was *Lord* Netherton? Why did he lie to me and say he was *Mr* Fanshawe?' Sophie glowered at her guardian. 'Oh, it was a great deal too bad of you! How can I ever hold my head up again?'

'But, my dear Sophie, I *did* try to tell you that he was not *Mr* Netherton; I recall very well that I made considerable efforts to correct your misimpression. But, if you remember, you hurried away rather precipitately, and you gave me no chance to effect a revision.'

'But you could have told me any time these last weeks!'

'Lord Netherton most particularly desired me not to.'

'But why? And why did you abide by his wishes? As my guardian I should have thought your first care would be to save me from such humiliation as I am now subject to!'

'There is indeed no humiliation, my dear,' Mr Moreton said earnestly.

'I feel there is, sir!' replied Sophie, blinking back the tears.

It was now their turn to dance down the set. Never can any young lady have opened her own come-out ball with a more furious countenance than did Sophie Neville that evening in Portland Square. More than one mamma sitting by the wall commented that it was obvious that her hair and her temper were in complete accord, and that they would be sorry for any man foolish enough to make an offer for her. But Sophie felt that if she stopped feeling furious for one instant, she would burst into tears of self-pity before them all. The humiliation!

Her next dance was with the Duke. He was his usual kindly self and Sophie made a tremendous effort to talk pleasantly with him. But he saw that something was wrong, and assumed all the burden of conversation, and she was duly grateful.

'You have been very kind, Your Grace,' Sophie said as he led her from the floor.

'If you need a confidant, my dear, I am at your service.'

'Oh, pray do not be too sympathetic, sir, or I may yet disgrace myself before you all!'

'Well, remember what I have said.'

Sophie smiled up at him gratefully and he led her back to her seat.

She was to stand up next with Sir Lionel. Lady Knight had insisted on their dancing together and had made constant references to it in the days leading up to the ball. With a very bad grace the two principals involved accepted the situation, and now Sir Lionel led her out with a face almost as grumpy as Sophie's own.

'Well, ma'am, what has put you about this time? Do not think it is any pleasure to me to stand up with such a crosspatch.'

Sophie, by now quite used to Sir Lionel's rudeness, was unsurprised by this remark and answered roundly, 'And it is no pleasure to me either, sir, you may be sure, but you know we both agreed to it at Lady Knight's insistence, so pray let us get it done with.'

They danced the whole set in silence, and when it was over, Sir Lionel led her off the floor in silence too. Lady Knight approached them, smiling happily.

'Such a pretty pair you make. But, Sophie, my dear, you look somewhat warm. Pray, Lionel, take her outside and find her some cordial.'

'Oh, I am very well, ma'am, I thank you. I am not at all thirsty,' said Sophie hastily.

'Nonsense, my dear. I can see that you need a little rest.'

'But I am to dance next with Sir Penistone.'

'I shall make your excuses to him. Now, off you go.'

Reluctantly the pair allowed themselves to be ushered out into a room which gave on to the little garden at the centre of the house. Lady Knight closed the door on them.

Sophie sat down on one of the sofas and folded her arms. 'I really can not think what my grandmamma is about. This is really exceedingly uncomfortable.'

Sir Lionel went and stood by the window looking out on to the garden.

'I assure you it is quite as disagreeable to me.'

'Why do you allow Lady Knight to do it, then?'

Sir Lionel turned to glare at Sophie.

'Come, Miss Neville, you are not so green as that!'

'What do you mean, sir?'

'The old girl holds the money-bags; that's what I mean, Miss Neville!'

'But—you have money of your own! The Knight fortune.'

'I have a very small allowance from a very small portion of the capital. The rest that old hellcat holds in a grip of iron!'

'You mean——' cried Sophie, surprised, not bothering to protest at the improper words applied to her grandparent.

'But I do not understand! You have money for your horses and your carriage and—and gambling—and—and—I know now what else! They can not be afforded on a very small allowance!'

'Oh, I am allowed the means to live as a gentleman—as long as I do as I am told! My aunt-in-law is not ungenerous with the Knight money, I grant you, provided she gets her own way in everything. When my uncle died, and left practically everything to his widow instead of to his heir, as he should have done, he served me the worst turn possible. There was not much Neville money when she married my uncle, I can tell you. Your grandmother had hung on to the control with a grip of steel.'

'And when do you receive the capital? Upon your marriage?'

'Not till Lady Knight chooses to give it to me, which will be when she dies.'

Sir Lionel stared moodily out into the garden.

'You—you will have to marry a rich wife then, will not you, sir?'

'If I marry away from the vixen's wishes, she may leave the lot to a charity school—or to you!'

Sophie ignored this rudeness and said very thoughtfully,

'But if you married a—*very* rich wife, that would not signify, would it?'

'She would have to be a female Croesus!'

After a pause, Sophie said airily, 'I collect there were very great fortunes made in the late war?'

'What do you mean?'

'Armaments and supplies—and things,' Sophie said vaguely. 'Would you *mind* a rich Cit's daughter?'

Sir Lionel turned and smiled slowly.

'By Jove, Miss Neville, it would serve her out!'

'What do you mean, sir?' Sophie said innocently.

But before Sir Lionel could reply, the door opened and in walked Lord Netherton.

'So here you are, Miss Neville; this is my dance, I think.'
And he bowed before Sophie, smiling genially. She looked up
at him, still much affronted.

'I do not recollect that I am engaged to you, sir.'

'Come, Miss Neville, you know it very well.'

'I assure you, sir, I do not!' cried Sophie, flaring up.

Sir Lionel moved towards them.

'You're Netherton, aren't you?'

Lord Netherton smiled smoothly, and gave a half-bow.

'Well,' went on Sir Lionel, 'let me give you some advice.
You'd do much better to steer clear of my stepcousin here.
She has the very devil of a temper. Quite likely to bring the
house down about your ears if she don't like you. You're new
in town, so I thought I'd warn you.'

And with that he walked out.

Sophie's face was a study. Her fury and rage were such
that had she been alone she would have stamped upon the
floor with a great deal of force. As it was, she merely ham-
mered with one fist on the sofa. She struggled for calm and
composure.

'Come, Miss Neville,' Lord Netherton said gently, offering
her his arm.

Sophie glared up at him, but his smile was so tender
that the angry riposte died on her lips, and instead she
gulped.

'Please, Miss Neville,' Lord Netherton said with genuine
feeling.

'I am supposed to be engaged to Sir Penistone Carver,'
Sophie murmured.

'I am certain I have just seen him standing up with Miss
Fennell—or was it my sister?'

Sophie looked up at him with quivering lips. She blinked
once or twice, then, without quite knowing what she did,
Sophie stood up and placed her hand on Lord Netherton's
proffered arm. They returned to the ballroom in silence.
They joined a set and Sophie stood, not knowing what she

felt. A myriad sensations chased through her mind, all painful, all unhappily out of place at a come-out ball. She gritted her teeth to hold back her tears.

'Have you nothing to say to me, Miss Neville?' Lord Netherton asked softly.

'Nothing, sir,' Sophie replied obstinately.

'You think I have deceived you; that is why you are angry with me.'

'*Think!*' she cried, hardly able to believe her ears. 'You did indeed deceive me, *Mr* Fanshawe!'

'Ah. But you must collect that I had until a very short time before indeed *been* Mr Fanshawe. I was but imperfectly used to my title.'

She glanced at him quickly, suspicious that he was laughing at her again. But Lord Netherton appeared perfectly serious.

'I inherited the title very unexpectedly from my third cousin—er—once removed.'

'I am afraid I am not acquainted with that degree of relationship, sir.'

'Nor was I, Miss Neville, but I assure you, I found such a relationship to exist in truth. One never hears about them, of course, unless a case of some such title as mine enters into the question. These titles have to be kept alive, you know, however little one may expect to receive them. I assure you, I had not got used to being *Lord Netherton* then. My cousin, who was Lord Netherton before me, lived in Venice. I had never met him—indeed, had barely heard of him—so I did not know he was unmarried and had no heirs. It was a great shock to me, I assure you!'

Sophie glanced quickly at Lord Netherton's face, and then as quickly looked away again.

'Indeed, to tell you the truth, Miss Neville, I knew very little of the title till it was dumped on my shoulders. Now I find that it is not even a particularly illustrious one. It is very disappointing!' Lord Netherton looked down at Sophie with a smile. 'I mean, it was not gained in battle, or anything glorious like that!'

Sophie was fully aware of the smile, but obstinately refused to look up.

'I hesitate to mention this before a lady, ma'am, but I have learnt, much to my chagrin, that it only came to the family because one of my ancestors was so complaisant as to marry one of King Charles the Second's numerous—er—friends. The King was so happy to have the lady taken off his hands that he gave my ancestor an earldom. In every other way, I am afraid, my ancestor was totally undistinguished. It is very lowering to one's self-esteem. The lady in question, I collect, had red hair. My sister has inherited it.'

'So I had remarked,' Sophie said shortly.

Lord Netherton continued to talk while Sophie had barely the heart to listen. She gazed down at her feet and felt more and more miserable. Here was *her* Mr Fanshawe at last, suddenly transformed into Lord Netherton, having played the most cruel and humiliating trick on her. And there was his sister, indeed dancing now with Sir Penistone Carver, and doubtless regaling him with a detailed account of the whole affair. Soon all London would be laughing at her. Oh, it was too cruel! Too much to be borne! The dance, which once she would have thought would have been her highest possible pleasure, in fact was one terrible purgatory. She was thankful when it was over, and she could escape to another partner.

She danced every dance and endeavoured to cast off her glooms and enjoy herself, but she could not throw off the idea that by now everyone in the room knew what had happened and was laughing at her behind their fans. Even the wicked Lord Buckland was unable to revive her much, but she flirted with him quite outrageously during the supper interval, and had never before enjoyed the game so little.

Sophie had been careful at first to avoid looking in the direction of Lord Netherton. But as time went on, she must have watched him out of the corner of her eye, for she was always perfectly aware in what part of the room he was to be found, and what young lady he chose to stand up with. She felt a furious resentment against them all. Part of her hoped desperately that he would ask her for another dance; she had none free, it is true—but—she would think of something! Another part of her, however, always told her furiously that she never wanted to look into those amused eyes again. She hated him! She despised him! He was, indeed, utterly despicable! And she was utterly humiliated.

She longed for her ball to be over. Even when she caught sight of herself in one of the many pier-glasses round the room, her beautiful dress and her hair, dressed to perfection in the Roman style by Yvette, no longer gave her any pleasure.

Lord Netherton did not approach her again. If, by some mysterious chance, their eyes did meet across the room, he would gaze at her with that winsome smile of his, and Sophie, to her mortification, found herself blushing very red. But he did not approach her, and she told herself that she was very glad.

And when at last the final guest had departed, Sophie rushed up to her bedroom and locked the door, and scalding tears of humiliation kept her awake for what was left of the night.

CHAPTER
ELEVEN

THE morning after her ball Sophie was afflicted with the headache and did not rise at her usual time. She refused to see Mr Moreton when he came up to enquire how she did, and only managed to raise a very small smile when Yvette came in with three huge bouquets, one from Lord Buckland, one from Lord Henchley and the third from Sir Peniston Carver.

A fourth basket of flowers arrived towards noon.

'The card says Netherton, miss. 'E's a new one, ain't 'e?' Yvette busied herself with setting up the flowers on a table. 'Very rich, by all I've 'eard. You're doing very well, miss.'

Sophie dissolved at once in tears.

'There, now, don't you take on so. You're only tired. It's quite natural.'

'It's—it's not that, Yvette,' sniffed Sophie.

'Well, I don't know what else it can be, after a successful ball like you've had. I've just read the notice in the *Post*, and it calls you "a regular beauty". There now! What do you say to that?'

'It's not a tribute to me, but to the Duke's strawberries and all your care,' Sophie said with an attempt at a smile.

'Good material to work on, miss,' Yvette returned briskly. 'Now, you try and get some sleep, or you'll look like a washed-out rag tonight.'

'I could not go anywhere tonight!'

'But you're expected, miss!' was all the reply she received.

In a few moments, the maid was back again with a note.

'Who is it from, Yvette?' asked Sophie without much interest. If Lord Netherton had intended communicating with her—— But she would not, could not care. She would never see him again. She could never, no never, face the world again. And it was all his fault! By tonight there would not remain one soul in London in ignorance of her humiliation, and there was nothing for her but to creep back to Mallowfield and spend the rest of her life in good and charitable works.

'Aren't you going to open it, then?'

When the maid handed it to her, Sophie saw at once by the writing on the envelope that it was from Camilla. She opened it with a slight feeling of guilt that she had not seen as much of her friend as she might have done since they had met again in London, and that she had not missed the intimacy.

The missive was penned in Camilla's usual spreading hand. Sophie could almost hear her friend speaking as she read her words:

'Dearest Sophie, I am in the very greatest haste, but I must tell you that when you next see me I shall be a married lady! Is not that exciting? Mr Martin—you remember the young man whom you saw at that concert—well, Mr Martin and I have come to an understanding. He says, Sophie dearest, that he is quite unable to live without me, and Oh! I am the happiest creature in London——No! In the whole world! Mamma has invited that horrid Sir Henry Thorley to call upon her and Papa tomorrow—no today—because I am writing this in the middle of the night—and you know what my Mamma is! So Mr Martin and I have decided that the only thing we can do is to elope to Gretna Green! Is not that the most exciting thing? I have always thought it so romantic, and can hardly believe that it is all going to come true for your friend, Camilla Hetherington. (That is the very last time I shall write that name!) P.S. Your ball was very brilliant, dear Sophie, but I could not enjoy it as I ought because I thought all the time of Mr Martin. I daresay you will make a great match now! C.'

Sophie read the letter through two or three times before she was certain that she understood it perfectly. Then she looked up at Yvette with wide, perturbed eyes.

'What is it, miss? Is something wrong?'

'I—I think something is very much wrong, Yvette. At least—I do not quite know how fashionable persons would view it—but I have always been told that——What—what do you think of—of people who—who elope, Yvette?'

'Oh ho! So that's what it is! Your bird-brained young friend is off to Gretna, is she? Well, it will do her no good in society, I can tell you. 'Alf the couples who go there are never married at all, and it is always——'

'Never married at all!' cried Sophie, horrified. 'Oh, do not say that, Yvette!'

'*And* it is always the woman who is ruined,' the maid continued firmly, 'like I was a-going to say—and serve her right for being so stupid!'

'Oh, Yvette, no! Never married at all! Do not say that—you frighten me more than ever! I am sure that Mr—that the person with whom——Oh!' Sophie went very pale. 'I am quite sure he is a complete gentleman!'

'*Gentlemen* do not take ladies off to Gretna Green,' Yvette said, more decidedly than ever. 'Don't you make no mistake about it, miss. It never ever did any woman any good going there, and if the news once gets known, then the lady's reputation's *gorn*—like dew in the sunshine, even if she *is* as white as driven snow, so to speak, which few enough of them are! You mark my words, miss, your friend'll——'

'Oh, stop, stop, Yvette! You terrify me!'

'What's that silly young ninny want to go for anyway?'

'Her—her mamma wishes her to marry Sir Henry Thorley.'

'That old roué! Even so, never did no good runnin' for Gretna.'

Sophie swung her legs out of the bed and stood up. 'I must stop her,' she declared, without having one coherent idea how she was to bring about such a desirable end. 'Help me dress, Yvette.'

'And 'ow do you propose to do that, miss?' the maid asked somewhat derisively. 'Stop 'er, I mean. Miss 'Etherington'll be well past Barnet, by now.'

'I do not know exactly, but I must try,' Sophie said more decidedly than her feelings warranted. Then she had an inspiration. She went over to the bell-pull and tugged it.

'*Now* what're you going to do?'

'Never mind. Just help me dress,' cried Sophie, dashing to the washstand and splashing her face with water.

'And 'ow's the 'eadache now?'

'Oh—it's—it's a little better, thank you,' mumbled Sophie as she dried her face vigorously. 'Now, be quick, Yvette; there's not a moment to lose!'

Then she sat down and held out one foot ready for Yvette to roll on the stocking.

'What you think you can do *I* can't imagine,' grumbled the maid pulling up the stocking and adjusting the garter. 'You'd be far better resting ready for this evening.'

'Oh, I could never do that!' Sophie cried, jumping up as soon as her stockings were in place and seizing her chemise. 'I should never be able to rest at all, thinking that my poor friend——'

Here she stopped while the garment was pulled over her head, which soon re-emerged with the curls somewhat more disordered.

'—Oh, why does not the girl hurry? I shall be ready in a moment!' she ended impatiently.

Just then there was a tap on the door and Sophie called hurriedly, 'Come in.'

The maid had barely time to enter the room before Sophie was giving her orders.

'Ah, there you are, Phyllis, what an age you have been!

Will you please give orders for the master's phaeton to be harnessed for me? I want the fastest horses in the stable.'

'The *master's* phaeton, miss?' the girl echoed, astonished.

'Yes! Yes!' Sophie answered impatiently. 'I need the very fastest horses available. Now hurry, girl, hurry!'

'Y—yes, miss,' said the maid disappearing.

'And what do you think *you're* going to do with the master's phaeton, I'd like to know?' demanded Yvette, looking at Sophie with arms akimbo.

'Go after Miss Camilla, of course,' Sophie answered distractedly, looking for her hairbrush, 'who is even now driving to her ruin,' she continued on a more dramatic note. 'A fine friend *I* should be if I left her to her fate. Oh, do do my hair, Yvette; I can see the brush in your hand all this time!'

'That I'll not, miss. I'll be no part to taking the master's blood horses. You could never handle them and it is stupid in you to try.'

'I am not going to drive them myself!' cried Sophie, amazed. 'No, Joshua must come with me. Oh, do do my hair, Yvette, or must I do it for myself?'

'The master never lets no one drive 'is chestnuts but 'imself,' Yvette said, brushing her mistress's hair with extra vigour born of disapproval. 'You just wait till 'e 'ears what you're about!'

'What else do you suggest?' answered Sophie reasonably. 'I have to travel as fast as possible, and Joshua is very safe.'

''E'll not do it,' said Yvette, 'e'd never dare!'

'We'll see,' said Sophie determinedly. 'Now, that's enough, Yvette. Help me with my dress. I'll wear the blue, sprigged one.'

The maid said nothing as she slipped the light muslin over Sophie's head, and attached the hooks at the back. Sophie waited impatiently till the dress was done, then she dashed over to the press and peered inside; quickly she pulled out a small, close-fitting bonnet and tied its ribbons firmly under her chin. Then she picked up her gloves and her reticule, glanced swiftly at herself in the cheval-glass, and with a quick glance at Yvette, who shook her head at her with a reluctant smile, she dashed from the room and down the stairs.

In the hall she peeped out of the window to see if the phaeton were before the door. The street was empty, so she rang the bell and waited with tapping foot till someone answered her summons. At last a footman appeared.

'Will you please tell them that I want the carriage brought round at once?' Sophie said imperiously.

The footman bowed and withdrew and Sophie paced the hall impatiently, thinking about Camilla and where she might be by now. In a few moments, the footman returned.

'Begging your pardon, miss, but you did say "the carriage", miss?'

'I gave orders at least a quarter of an hour ago for the master's phaeton to be harnessed. I want Joshua to drive it for me.'

The footman's eyes flickered for a moment, but he said nothing other than 'Very good, miss', before hastily withdrawing. Sophie resumed her pacing, but instead of the expected sound of horses' hooves in the street outside, there came at last the sound of voices in the servants' passage, and soon the footman was back again with Joshua himself close behind him.

'Well, Joshua,' Sophie began, 'what is this? I am in a very great hurry to be off. What is the matter?'

'Oi dursn't do it, miss.'

'What do you mean?'

'Oi dursn't 'arness the master's phaeton, miss; not wi'out 'e gi'es me the orders hisself.'

'But *I* have given the orders, Joshua!'

'Oi'm very sorry, miss!' the groom answered unhappily. 'The carriage, yes, Oi'll bring that round and cum wi' you wi' pleasure, wherever you wants to go, but—not the master's phaeton, miss. I dursn't!' he repeated piteously. 'Truly, I dursn't, miss!'

'Are you refusing to obey my orders?' cried Sophie furiously, staring at the man, her face flaming with anger and mortification.

But the groom was saved having to make an answer by a loud peal from the front door bell. The footman glanced at Sophie and she nodded to him. The man straightened his shoulders and went with measured tread to open the door.

In a moment Sophie heard Lord Netherton's familiar tones enquiring if she were at home. Her mind was thrown into even more of a whirl. Of all the people in the world, he was the one she least wished to see, but her friend's predicament was now uppermost in her mind, and she did not permit her own feelings to sway her now.

The footman had only time to say, 'I will see, my lord; if your lordship would be so good as to——' when Sophie swept forward, put her hand on Lord Netherton's arm, and drew him swiftly down the steps and on to the pavement.

'Do you know the way to Gretna Green, my lord?' she hissed urgently, anxious that the footman, still waiting by the door above should not hear her.

Whatever his eyes may have expressed, Lord Netherton's voice was admirably controlled as he answered her in an imitation of her own tone.

'You have only to say the word, Miss Neville.'

'Then let us go,' she answered in the same manner, and picking up her skirts, she stepped towards the curricle standing at the edge of the pavement.

Without another word, Lord Netherton handed her in, and in another moment was seated beside her. The little tiger let go the horses' heads, jumped up behind, and in a trice they were trotting smartly out of the square.

'I am very glad that your horses are so fresh, my lord,' Sophie said, eyeing the glossy flanks of the animals in front of her, which were clearly some of the best ever to come out of Tattersall's.

'My dear Miss Neville, had I known that you wished to

embark upon such a long journey, I should have come more adequately prepared—with sustenance, and pistols and so on.'

'Pistols!' Sophie turned to look at Lord Netherton in apprehensive astonishment. 'Why should we need pistols?'

'There are some very wild places once we are north of Barnet.'

'I—I hope it may not be necessary to go so far!'

'Do not worry, Miss Neville; *I* will protect you,' Lord Netherton answered with a dramatic look. 'But if you wish to reach Gretna, ma'am, I assure you that this is the normal route to take,' he went on in his normal voice.

'Oh, but *I* do not wish to go to Gretna!'

Lord Netherton looked at her, a very disappointed expression on his face.

'Forgive me, Miss Neville, clearly I have quite misunderstood you. I thought you said——'

'Oh, no! It is *my friend*—Miss Camilla Hetherington—who has already set out for Gretna, and I am trying to catch up with her to stop her. I can not allow her to ruin herself, even if it is to escape from Sir Henry Thorley. You *do* understand, do not you?'

'Oh, yes, I quite see that,' answered Lord Netherton, guiding the curricle round an obstruction in the road with great dexterity. 'But when did your friend—and her—her partner—set out? They may already have travelled a considerable way. We may not be in time.'

'She has gone with a Mr Martin. And I do not think they will have gone so very far. I received my friend's note only a short time ago, and Mr Martin did not seem to me to be —well, I do not think he will be able to hire the very fastest horses. I wanted to go after them in Sir Lionel's phaeton, but the groom was too cowardly to harness it for me,' went on Sophie indignantly. 'So I am very glad you appeared when you did, my lord, or I might never have caught up with poor Camilla.'

'I am very glad to be able to be of service to you, Miss Neville,' Lord Netherton said very genuinely, glancing at her with a little smile. 'Did you say your friend was escaping from Sir Henry Thorley?'

She nodded. 'Lady Hetherington wishes her to marry him, but Camilla is in love with Mr Martin.'

'I would not have thought Thorley a suitable choice for a young girl. He has been looking for an heiress these two seasons past.'

'But—but I thought he was very rich! I know Lady Hetherington thinks so; but I did tell her once I had seen him gambling very high. She did not like that; she is a great Evangelical, and regularly goes to hear Mr Fenton. But perhaps Sir Henry's title persuaded her. Lady Hetherington so wants Camilla to be a lady.'

'Lady Hetherington sounds a most formidable matron if she can enjoy Mr Fenton! But I promise you, Thorley has already run through a great part of his fortune and looks to refurbish it.'

'Then you must tell Lady Hetherington that! Poor Camilla can only be happy with Mr Martin, and she does not mind at all that she will not be a lady or anything!'

They were nearing the outskirts of the town now, and were able to travel more quickly. Lord Netherton concentrated on guiding the horses through the remaining traffic as expeditiously as possible and very soon they were out in the open country and moving along at a spanking pace.

They stopped at Mr Horne's establishment at Barnet to change the horses and made enquiries about the young couple they were following, but none of the ostlers they spoke with could give them any help. Not one remembered a young couple travelling alone, and Sophie and Lord Netherton had to proceed accompanied by a certain amount of doubt as to whether their quarry was in fact on their route.

They left the tiger behind at Barnet, partly so that he could jog Lord Netherton's blood-horses back to London when they were rested, and partly to make more space in the curricle, 'for as you can see, Miss Neville, this sort of conveyance is not really suited to the errand upon which we are engaged, and if we do come up with your friends, I am afraid we will have a very squashed journey back—that is, if we can persuade them to return with us.'

However, in the event, their journey outwards ended much sooner than might have been expected. They had travelled only some three miles from Barnet, and were just about to cross an extensive grassy common studded with a myriad gorse-bushes in full flower, when they caught sight of a chaise stationary under the shade of some trees some little distance from the track. A young woman was seated on the ground and a man appeared to be inspecting the hoof of one of the horses.

Sophie put her hand on Lord Netherton's arm,

'My lord,' she said, drawing his attention to the couple, 'I am not sure, but that looks like——'

Lord Netherton slowed the horses and turned them towards the chaise.

'It is! It is Camilla!' cried Sophie, when they were closer. 'Camilla!' she called out, waving vigorously.

The young woman looked up, then jumped to her feet and started running towards them.

'Oh, Sophie! Sophie! How vewy glad I am that you are come!'

Lord Netherton stopped the curricle and without waiting for him to help her, Sophie jumped down and she and Camilla flung their arms about each other.

'How did you find us?' Camilla wept, tears of relief streaming down her cheeks. 'Oh, I have been sitting here an hour or more waiting to be murdered!'

'I set out as soon as I could, Camilla. Your note put me in such a fright. Lord Netherton was so kind as to bring me after you for I could not——'

'Lord Netherton! Is that Lord Netherton!' Camilla

asked with huge eyes, turning to look at the young man in question.

'I do not know of any other,' Sophie answered dismissively. 'But if he had not arrived at the very moment——'

'You amaze me, Sophie, weally you do!' cried Camilla, shaking her head.

'And you amaze me, Camilla,' her friend returned somewhat impatiently. 'I can not think what you are about, ruining yourself like this, for Yvette says that would surely happen, and you would not like that at all, you know!'

'Oh, do not scold, Sophie! I should not have cared a bit for that if only I could have been quickly mawwied to Mr Martin, but one of the horses we got at Barnet has gone lame, and we have been sitting here for I do not know how long, waiting for highwaymen to come and cut our thwoats! Oh, I can not tell you what a fwight I have been in, and how vewy thankful I am that you are come now!'

Over Camilla's shoulder Sophie caught sight of Lord Netherton and Mr Martin, and to her surprise the two men were greeting each other like old friends.

'Miss Neville,' called Lord Netherton, starting to walk back towards her, 'is not this the most astonishing coincidence? Dick Martin and I are old friends; we live near each other in Berkshire and have been acquainted since we were boys! Allow me to present Mr Richard Martin to you. Dick, this is—Miss Neville—of Mallowfield.'

Sophie was acutely conscious of the slightest hesitation which she had heard in his lordship's voice, and now that the purpose of her helter-skelter scramble along the Gretna road had been achieved, she was suddenly very conscious of her own situation. But she extended her hand graciously to Mr Martin and smiled and curtsied. Mr Martin seemed to be quite as pleasant upon a second inspection as he had looked when she first saw him at the Duchess of Milton's subscription concert.

'I am very glad to meet you at last, sir,' she said.

'And I am delighted to meet you, Miss Neville. Miss Hetherington—Camilla—has told me so much about you.'

Sophie then presented Lord Netherton to Camilla, and after much exclaiming on the extraordinary circumstance of the two men being such friends, it was decided that it was high time that they all returned to London.

'I confess, Michael, that I am extremely glad things have turned out as they have,' Mr Martin said ruefully. 'I did not care for this adventure one bit, but there seemed nothing else for it when we knew that Thorley was to come to speak with Sir Paul this afternoon. We only decided upon it suddenly before your ball, Miss Neville, and I am afraid we were not able to prepare as we should.'

'Well, we shall be able to get some fast horses in Barnet and be back in London late this afternoon,' Lord Netherton said comfortably. 'Then no one need know anything about your adventure. You could say, Miss Hetherington, that you went for a drive and one of the horses went lame and that delayed you. All that would be perfectly true. Unless you have also left a note for your mother, Lady Hetherington?'

'Oh, no! I sent one only to Sophie. I was too afwaid my mamma would catch up with us if she knew early enough where we had gone. And I thought that by the time she had thought to ask Sophie if she knew where I was, we should be too far away for her to catch us.'

'And what will you do when you get home, Camilla?' Sophie asked. 'I am afraid Lady Hetherington will be very angry, even if she does not discover that you set out for Gretna. A lame horse is hardly likely to endear Mr Martin to her.'

'I do not know,' Camilla wept, 'but I know I shall never mawwy anyone but Mr Martin,' and she clung very tightly to that young man's arm.

They now began to make their way back to Barnet, Sophie and Camilla seated in Lord Netherton's curricle with Lord

Netherton leading the horses, and Mr Martin leading the hired chaise.

'What, exactly, is Lady Hetherington's objection to you, Dick?' Lord Netherton asked his friend. 'As far as I know, you are upright and honest, and not at all likely to beat your wife!'

'I am suffering from precisely those same disadvantages that dogged you last year when you were in pursuit of Miss Woodville,' Mr Martin returned with a short laugh. 'To wit, lack of money, lack of prospects, and lack of a title! And I am afraid I am not like to be got out of *my* difficulties by such luck as came your way, Michael; after all, *I* am only a second son!'

Lord Netherton had shot his friend a warning glance when he mentioned the name of Miss Woodville, and the look was not lost upon Sophie. As soon as she had heard the strange young lady's name, she had experienced an extraordinary mixture of feelings, which started with dismayed surprise and ended with deep conviction that she would dislike the unknown Miss Woodville exceedingly were she ever to meet her. She felt an irrational anger against Lord Netherton and stared hard at the back of that gentleman's hat, but most determinedly he did not look back towards her. Instead he said to his friend,

'You have not got a curacy yet then, I collect?'

Mr Martin shook his head. 'No. You know how it is, Michael. I have applied to the Duke of Mayfair, who is the patron of my father's living, but he has got nothing of any worth in hand now. Although I do not consider myself extravagant, fifty pounds a year, I think, would be quite impossible.'

'I should think so too,' agreed Lord Netherton warmly. 'But I may be able to help you. I understand that I have a living in my gift—in Dorset, not far from Mallowfield. It has to be filled, and you are very welcome to it if you would like it. I believe it is a good one, and has a very pleasant parsonage-house. Miss Neville,' he said, turning round at last, 'you may perhaps know Overcombe Rectory? It is a very pretty place, is not it?'

Sophie's thoughts had been entirely engaged with Miss Woodville. Now, when Lord Netherton suddenly appealed to her, she brought her mind back to the immediate situation with an effort.

'I am sorry, my lord,' she answered stiffly, 'I did not hear what you said.'

'Oh, *I* know Overcombe!' exclaimed Camilla. 'It is—it is the most delightful parsonage-house ever, my lord!'

'I am so glad you like it,' Lord Netherton smiled. He glanced swiftly at Sophie's stony face, then turned back to his friend again, and went on to tell him more of the Overcombe living.

CHAPTER
TWELVE

IT was late in the afternoon when they reached London once more, and it was decided that it would be best to go to Portland Square first to see if Lady Hetherington had been there to make enquiries about her errant daughter. Sophie had hardly spoken a word all the way home, answering only when spoken to. She had received a very severe blow.

After her ball, she had been quite certain that she could never face Lord Netherton or his sister again, so humiliated did she feel by the trick they had played upon her. But after he had been so instrumental in helping her chase after Camilla, she had begun to think that, after some years had elapsed, she might be able to forgive him in spite of everything.

Now all this was changed. It seemed that Lord Netherton was only a philanderer after all. Pursuing Miss Woodville, indeed! How lucky that her eyes had been opened in time!

Now they were arrived outside her grandmother's house in Portland Square and, disdaining Lord Netherton's proffered hand, Sophie jumped down and walked stiffly up the steps to ring the bell. They were soon all inside, and she was just enquiring if Lady Hetherington had called that afternoon, when Mr Moreton came hurrying into the hall.

'Thank heaven you are returned safely, Sophie; I have been extremely worried ever since Yvette told me that you had gone off in such a hurry. As for you, sir,' he went on, turning to Mr Martin, 'it seems to me that the sooner you leave this young lady alone, the better! The footman will show you out directly.'

'Mr Moreton, sir,' said Lord Netherton hurriedly, stepping forward, 'the whole affair has been a sad mistake, but do please let me explain things to you. I have known Dick Martin for years, and he is not at all as you think him, I do assure you! May not we go in and let us tell you everything?'

'If I had not known it was you Sophie had rushed off with, my lord, I should have had every constable in the country alerted!' Mr Moreton said, still clearly put out. 'Really, Miss Hetherington, I would not have thought even you would be guilty of such an addle-pated scheme!'

Camilla started to sniff at this, and Mr Martin took her hand comfortingly. Mr Moreton led the way into the small salon.

'Well, well, you had better tell me all about it. I must confess, my lord,' he said turning to Lord Netherton, 'your presence was my only security. It was lucky that John recognised you; I thought at first it was that rogue Buckland that Sophie was off with.'

Sophie said nothing, but looked down at her toes.

Lord Netherton asked, 'Have you informed Lady Hetherington of what has happened, sir?'

'I have not, my lord. I hoped your mission would be successful before her ladyship needed to be apprised of what had occurred.'

Mr Moreton gazed round at the four young people.

'Well?' he said, sternly.

'Miss Hetherington feared that her family were about to force her into a marriage which she could not like,' began Lord Netherton. 'And I must say, sir, I see her point. No young woman of my acquaintance could welcome a marriage with Sir Henry.'

'And which Sir Henry is this?' asked Mr Moreton, relaxing only slightly.

'Sir Henwy Thorley,' Camilla wailed, tears welling up in

her eyes anew. 'Mamma wants me to be a lady, but I do not care a jot for that, for Sir Henwy is an *old* man, and I do so want to be mawwied to Dick!' And Camilla turned to Mr Martin, who put his arms round her.

'Sir Henry Thorley!' Mr Moreton glanced across at Lord Netherton.

'*Exactly*,' his lordship said. 'You have doubtless heard a great deal about Sir Henry, sir.'

'And do you have the means to keep a wife?' Mr Moreton asked severely, turning to Mr Martin.

'*I* have promised Dick a living, sir,' Lord Netherton answered. 'Overcombe, near Mallowfield, is now in my gift. I have known Dick all my life, sir, and can vouch for his respectability.'

'A clergyman!' exclaimed Mr Moreton, his eyebrows rising.

'Mr Martin, Dick's father, has a living in Berkshire, near my own home. His is of a most respectable old family, sir, as His Grace of Mayfair can attest also. His Grace is the patron of Mr Martin's living, sir.'

'Well, it does seem as if the whole matter has been very sadly managed,' began Mr Moreton, with a sharp look at Mr Martin who bowed in acknowledgement. 'I know, sir.'

'Oh, do not be cwoss with Dick, Mr Moreton; it was all my idea. He did not want to do it at all, but I made him!' Camilla cried.

It was at that moment that the footman appeared to announce that Lady Hetherington was arrived, and asking to have speech with Miss Neville.

'Oh! Mamma!' Camilla shrieked, and clung to Mr Martin.

'Do I collect,' Mr Moreton asked quietly, 'that Lady Hetherington is as yet unaware that you had set out for—for the north?' Mr Moreton looked from Camilla to Mr Martin.

Mr Martin answered quietly, 'That is so, sir.'

'I will not go back and mawwy Sir Henwy!' Camilla shrieked. 'I will not! I will kill myself first!'

'I do not think such drastic action will be necessary, my dear,' said Mr Moreton with quite kindly exasperation. 'I suggest that we give her ladyship the impression that you have merely made a normal social call here.'

He looked round at them all questioningly, and they all nodded.

'That is what we had thought would be best, sir,' said Lord Netherton.

'Please show her ladyship in at once,' Sophie uttered in a small voice to the waiting footman.

The man bowed and withdrew, and in a few moments Lady Hetherington sailed into the room looking distraught. She saw Sophie and made straight towards her. Without bothering with greetings, her ladyship started agitatedly.

'Is Camilla here, Sophie? She is not to be found in Merriott Square, and I had thought she was visiting Miss Sanderson: you may have met her, Sophie, she lives in Welbeck Street. At least, Camilla gave me the distinct impression that she was to spend the day there, I am sure. I had expected her back this afternoon for—for a very particular caller, but she did not return, though we waited for her. But when a short time ago Miss Sanderson called to enquire after Camilla, you can imagine how I felt then! So I am come round directly to you, for if she is not with you, then I fear she is quite disgraced, and it is all the fault of that dreadful Mr Martin!'

Everyone had risen to their feet when Lady Hetherington had entered the room, and now, as she paused to draw breath, Sophie said quietly, 'But Camilla *is* here, your ladyship. See.'

And Sophie motioned to where Camilla and Mr Martin were standing behind Lady Hetherington. Camilla was looking at her mother with very frightened eyes, clinging tightly the while to Mr Martin's hand.

Lady Hetherington turned round and saw her daughter clinging to the despised young man's hand. Her relief at seeing her safe was immediately swept away by her fury at seeing her in this particular situation.

'Camilla! Come here at once! How dare you, sir!' she uttered in a wrathful voice, glaring formidably at Mr Martin. 'Camilla, I order you to leave that young man's side immediately!' She turned to Mr Moreton with an angry look. 'I would not have thought, sir, that you would have permitted this—this assignation here. Sophie, I know, has not sense enough to see that it is wrong, but I had thought better of you, sir!'

Sophie gasped at this unexpected attack, and felt her face go scarlet. But Mr Moreton said in a very quiet voice, 'You are quite mistaken, ma'am, I assure you. There has been no question of assignation here. Miss Hetherington has called to see my stepdaughter, who, I may add, has been brought up to know the difference between right and wrong, and would never contemplate such an action as you have suggested.'

His tone was such that Lady Hetherington wavered.

'I am sorry, Sophie, I should not have said that. Pray ascribe it to my present agitation. But as for you, miss,' she went on, turning back to her daughter who was still clinging to Mr Martin's arm, 'if you do not leave that young man's side this instant, I will cast you off, and neither your father nor I nor any of your family will ever speak to you again!'

'Mamma!' wailed Camilla, wavering.

'Your father and I have come to an arrangement with —with Sir Henry Thorley. It is a most advantageous match to you in every way. I will not have you jeopardising your whole future for a—a nobody!'

'Sir Henry Thorley!' exclaimed Mr Moreton. 'Is that the person you have in mind for your daughter, ma'am?'

'Indeed it is, sir!'

'Well,' said Mr Moreton deliberately, 'I can tell you, Lady Hetherington, that I would not permit Sophie to marry Sir Henry Thorley if he were the last man on earth!'

'I do not suppose Sir Henry has showed the least interest in Sophie!' her ladyship retorted.

'I am happy to say not. Sir Henry is well known to be a fortune-hunter, having almost entirely dissipated his own in gambling. I am surprised that Sir Paul, at least, has not heard rumours of the gentleman's true circumstances.'

'*I* have never heard anything to his discredit,' Lady Hetherington asserted, a trace of doubt beginning to enter her voice.

'What! you have never heard that he is one of the greatest gamblers in London!' cried Mr Moreton in amazement. 'I had thought everyone in society had known that! I assure you, if Sophie were his wife I should never have a moment's peace, thinking her very home might be gambled away, and she and her children left penniless in the world!'

'I—I did try to warn you, ma'am,' put in Sophie, '—at the subscription concert when first you told me your plans.'

'I did not know it was so bad,' murmured Lady Hetherington with a worried look.

'And—Mr Martin does not gamble at all, do you, sir?' Sophie went on. 'And he is known to His Grace of Mayfair who would help him if he can, and—and Lord Netherton has promised Mr Martin a good living, have not you, sir?' she added, unable to raise her eyes to look Lord Netherton straight in the face.

'Lord Netherton?' her ladyship demanded, turning to him.

Lord Netherton bowed. 'I think we did once meet in Dorset, ma'am, in this spring.'

'Oh yes, indeed, my lord; how could I possibly forget it?' Lady Hetherington cried, with something of a social gush. 'Pray forgive me, sir,' she went on, 'I did not see you there at first. You are—acquainted with—Mr Martin, then?' Her ladyship pronounced the name with extreme distaste.

'I have known Dick all my life, ma'am. We are great friends. You would not find a better fellow anywhere. Why, if he had taken it into his head to marry my sister instead of the charming Miss Hetherington, nothing would have given me greater pleasure.'

'You are very kind, my lord,' simpered Lady Hetherington. 'Of course, what you say carries very great weight with me, but—Sir Henry—he did seem such a thorough-going gentleman.'

'I assure you, ma'am, everything Mr Moreton has told you is true. Last season Sir Henry even persuaded the sister of—well, I will not mention the lady's name, it would not be fair, but I can tell you that the lady in question bears one of the very greatest names in England—well, he persuaded this lady, I say, to elope with him, but fortunately they were brought back in time. Oh yes, Sir Henry is growing to be a very desperate man, though, living in the country as you do, you may not have heard of it.'

'I can hardly believe it!' cried Lady Hetherington, sitting down suddenly. Then she caught sight of Camilla and Mr Martin. 'You are a clergyman, sir?' she asked, addressing Mr Martin.

He bowed.

'On which side of the great divide, sir?' she went on sternly.

'I tend towards the Evangelicals, ma'am.'

'Humph! I am glad to hear it! Well, I do not know what your father will say to this news of Sir Henry, Camilla; I confess it has upset me very much. We shall certainly have to make more enquiries about him, though I *did* think him so very suitable.' Her ladyship rose. 'We will not take up any more of your time, sir,' she said to Mr Moreton. 'Come, Camilla. I hope we shall see something of you in Merriott Square, my lord.'

Lord Netherton bowed.

'Goodbye, Sophie,' her ladyship continued, 'your ball last night was very tolerable, very tolerable indeed. But you *must* learn not to scowl so much; you will never get a husband that way. Mr Martin, you may show me to my carriage.'

And without waiting for the footman to be summoned, Lady Hetherington swept out, followed by her daughter and Mr Martin.

When the door was closed behind them, the three remaining behind looked at each other, or rather two of them did; Sophie for her part glanced at her stepfather, and then kept her eyes fixed firmly on her slippers, resolutely refusing to meet Lord Netherton's eyes.

'Well, my lord,' said Mr Moreton with the hint of a smile, 'do you think we have sufficiently cooked Sir Henry's goose?'

'I shall make certain of it, sir,' Lord Netherton said positively. 'I shall call upon her ladyship in Merriott Square, and make quite certain of the matter.'

'I admit I can scarcely pity the man,' said Mr Moreton, 'but Lady Hetherington has run after titles for all her daughters. I am sure she must have blinded herself to the rumours; I can not think that she has not heard them. And though I think Miss Camilla is the silliest goose that ever lived, I could not wish Sir Henry upon her. Mr Martin will do for her very well, though I cannot say that I think your friend has got much of a bargain!'

'But she is very pretty, sir!' protested Lord Netherton.

'But quite empty-headed. Still, if that is what he wants——' Mr Moreton looked from Lord Netherton to Sophie, who had not once looked up since Lady Hetherington and her party had left. Mr Moreton returned his gaze to Lord Netherton with questioning eyebrows. That gentleman gave a slight nod, and Mr Moreton rose.

'If you will excuse me, my lord, I have some letters that I ought to finish to catch this evening's mail.'

'Of course, sir.'

'Sophie, my dear,' Mr Moreton added, looking at his stepdaughter, 'I think you have acted very well in this matter of your friend, and Lord Netherton has been extremely kind to give up so much of his time to help you. He did not know that he was chasing after his own friend when you set out, did he?'

Mr Moreton left the room and closed the door carefully behind him. Sophie continued to look down at her toes, but suddenly she saw Lord Netherton's boots a little distance from her own silk slippers.

'Well, Miss Neville?' she heard him say.

'My stepfather is quite right, my lord,' she managed to get out. 'I must thank you very much for aiding me today. Camilla owes you a great deal, though I do not suppose she will ever realise it!'

'I was only too glad to be able to help *you*—Sophie.'

Her name, she thought, sounded quite delightfully on Lord Netherton's lips, but this thought was immediately followed by the recollection of Miss Woodville, and then every pleasant feeling was chased away.

Sophie's shoulders stiffened.

'I was not aware that we had reached such familiar terms, my lord,' she said pointedly, in a stiff little voice.

'After we have travelled half-way across England together? And now saved your friend, and mine, from the results of a very great indiscretion, which would have doubtless meant their social ruin? Oh, come, Sophie, do not be so cold with me.'

'Lord Netherton,' said Sophie coldly, looking up with flashing eyes, 'I am aware that you have assisted me very greatly today, and on my friend's behalf, I am grateful.'

She paused to draw breath, and Lord Netherton said,

'What I did, I did for you, Sophie. I did not care a—a button what happened to your friend.'

Sophie took no notice, but went on with what she had been about to say before.

'I would remind you, sir, that previously you have made me the laughing-stock of London, and for that I do not find it so easy to be grateful!'

'The laughing-stock of——! What can you mean?'

'You know very well what I mean, *Mr Fanshawe*!' Sophie retorted, feeling crosser than ever as she saw Lord Netherton's smiling face. Surely the man should feel *some* shame for the way he had used her! But apparently not! '*You* will be able to dine out on the whole story for months; it will be a very good dinner-table joke. But—I—*I*—will never be able to show my face in London society again without having a hundred people tittering at my expense behind their fans. And now I find that—in addition to all this—you are nothing but a—a common philanderer!'

'Philanderer!' repeated Lord Netherton, looking exceedingly surprised.

'Yes, philanderer, sir,' cried Sophie, warming to her theme. 'All last season you were chasing after Miss—Miss Woodville, and when she had too much sense and would have none of you, you thought *this* season you would have some sport with *me*!'

Lord Netherton threw back his head and gave a shout of laughter.

'So *that* is what has been the matter with you all this time! My dear, silly, *stupid* little ninny, Miss Woodville never meant anything——'

'Silly, *stupid* little——!' Sophie gasped, jumping up, almost overcome with rage. 'How dare you, sir! Oh, how dare you sir! You have no right to speak to me in that fashion! Oh, I should have known you for what you were long ago. Last year you had no money and chased after heiresses; this season the situation is changed, and so you think you will enjoy yourself at the expense of what you doubtless think is an inexperienced country girl! Well, I have seen through you, sir! You are quite as bad as Sir Henry Thorley! No, worse! My stepfather has been as much taken in by you as ever Lady Hetherington was by Sir Henry. Oh, to think that he ever contemplated——'

'My dear Miss Neville,' Lord Netherton interrupted a trifle impatiently, 'you really are talking a lot of nonsense.

You sound like a selection of purple speeches from all the worst circulating-library novels that you have ever read—and badly cobbled together at that! You know perfectly well that I am nothing at all like Sir Henry Thorley; *he* would not have put up with your silliness for one instant, I promise you. Oh, I have been warned by several people about your impossible temper, but because I had never seen it, I had thought you had grown out of it. That is, till last night—when you had not even the grace to dance at your own ball with a smiling face; you were, I must tell you quite plainly, a very sad hostess. Tantrums may be all very well in the country, but they do not do in London society, I assure you.

'It is a great pity Mr Moreton was not a great deal stricter with you. If you had run away and caused *me* the worry—and pain—that you caused him, I should have taken you home and locked you up and kept you on bread and water, and not let you come out at all. So, for goodness' sake, Sophie, stop being a silly goose and behave in a civilised manner. I confess I am uncommonly tired of——'

Sophie had been staring at Lord Netherton, hardly able to believe her ears. No one had ever spoken so to her before—with that mixture of impatience and patronage.

'And I am uncommonly tired of your speaking to me so,' Sophie blazed. 'You are quite the most insufferable person I have ever met, you—you—you——' Sophie was quite incoherent with rage.

A slight smile appeared on Lord Netherton's lips which enraged her even more.

'You—brute!' she breathed, and drew back her hand to deliver a stinging blow to his cheek; but Lord Netherton caught her wrist in a steel-like grip, and held it in the air for a moment while he gave her a long, cool, appraising look; then he dropped her wrist and turned on his heel.

'Yes, go, you—you bully!' Sophie shouted after him. 'I never want to see you again! You are no gentleman to treat a lady so, for all you have acquired a great title. You have certainly not inherited the manners to go with it!'

Lord Netherton did not turn or pause, but went out of the room and closed the door quietly behind him.

Sophie stared at the closed door, hardly able to believe what had happened. She stood in the salon panting, but otherwise unmoving; but when she heard the great front door open and then close, she rushed upstairs to her bedroom and flung herself on her bed in a paroxysm of weeping.

CHAPTER
THIRTEEN

SOPHIE did not know how long she had lain there when she heard a quite distinct shriek from her grandmother. It came up quite clearly to the bedroom storey. Sophie sat up in bed startled and strained her ears. Another shriek, similar to the first one, assailed her. Then she heard the sound of footsteps coming quickly up the stairs, and shortly afterwards the sound of Mr Moreton's voice saying pantingly, 'But, ma'am, I beg you—it is not——'

The footsteps continued up to the bedroom floor. Sophie heard Mr Moreton again expostulating, but he was much impeded by his hurrying ascent. There was a rustle of silken skirts in the corridor outside, and in a moment Lady Knight swept into the room, clearly in a state of extreme agitation.

'It is all your fault, you ungrateful girl!' she began, glaring at Sophie.

'But—but what have I done, ma'am?' cried Sophie, suddenly conscious of the headache brought on by all her weeping. She winced at her grandmother's strident tones.

'I told you to be pleasant with Sir Lionel!' Lady Knight said angrily. 'You know perfectly well that I wished you two to make a match of it! And what do you do, you unfeeling child? You ungrateful girl? Instead of doing as I bid you—for your own good, I may say, for without a dowry you stand no chance at all of making a great match, so do not think it—you do nothing but quarrel with him, and upset him, and cast him off with the most ill-mannered behaviour, and make no effort at all to do as I bid you—so do not think that the Neville fortune will come to you automatically, for it will not.

I have entire control of it to do as I wish with it—and I shall certainly think again before I leave a penny to you, you wicked, ungrateful baggage—and after all the trouble I have taken to give you the very best ball of the season!—And the expense! You have no consideration at all for my feelings! You have done exactly as you pleased—you have had no thought for me at all! After all I have done!'

Sophie stared at her grandmother. Never had she seen her so out of control before, and dimly, in the back of her mind, the sight of the red curls shaking angrily, and the sound of the strident voice, reminded her of something. She was appalled by the flood of invective that was pouring over her head, and was quite unable to think of any words with which to defend herself. Not that she did not feel all the injustice of her grandmother's accusations. It was *she*, not Sophie herself, who should be blamed! To have the idea that she should marry the more than odious Sir Lionel! Why, the very thought was so repulsive, it made her squirm just to think of it!

But she remained mute and let the tirade pour over her head. She and her grandmother faced each other, the older woman her face a mask of anger, Sophie herself aggrieved and showing it—this terrible scene on top of all that she had already suffered that day! It was all too much! It was more than she could bear! But now she could hear Mr Moreton nearing the top of the staircase. Surely he would come to her defence?

Lady Knight had gained her second wind and had begun again.

'After all I have done for you! After all I have done for you, wretched girl! My poor Lionel! My poor, foolish Lionel! It is all your fault,' she repeated, stopping to glare at Sophie once more. 'Oh, the injustice of it, after all I have done! The humiliation of it! I do not know that I can bear it. He will never have another easy night. Driven into the arms of that woman!'

'What woman?' cried Sophie, now bewildered.

Mr Moreton now appeared in the doorway as Lady Knight sank into an upholstered chair and beat her hands upon the arms. Her face was contorted with fury, and suddenly Sophie saw how old her grandmother must be. There were no youthful mannerisms about her now. She now looked the ageing woman she was, with her incongruous auburn curls shaking angrily round her enamelled face.

'But what have I done, ma'am?' Sophie asked again. She looked questioningly at Mr Moreton, who came over to the bed and, seating himself upon it, took Sophie's hand and whispered,

'Lady Knight has had a very great shock, Sophie. You must not mind what she says.'

Her grandmother, meanwhile, vouchsafed no answer to Sophie's question, but instead said in venomous tones, 'That odious female! That—brazen creature! How dare she? Oh, how dare she!'

'But what is it, ma'am? Can not you tell me what has so upset you?'

Sophie looked to Mr Moreton for explanation, but before he could say a word, Lady Knight burst out again.

'Sir Lionel and—and that woman! That creature—married!'

'Good God! Do you mean Lady Ball, ma'am?'

'I do indeed, miss! And no word to me of it! She—Lady Ball—a fishmonger's widow—for that is all her precious Sir Herbert was at first—a fishmonger! And she to be Lady Knight! Oh, I cannot bear it! The shame! I can not bear the shame! That I should have to give place to her! A *nouvelle riche!* Lady Ball! Oh! It is all too much! It is all your fault!'

'My fault, ma'am?'

'Indeed, yes, miss! *All* your fault! If you had married Sir Lionel as I wished, all this would not have come about!'

'But, ma'am,' said Sophie, endeavouring to speak reasonably, though her head felt as if it were splitting, 'but, ma'am, it seems to me that Sir Lionel has always been attached to Lady Ball. *That* is why he never expressed the slightest interest in me. In fact, not to put too fine a point upon it, he was always quite shockingly offensive and rude to me! I tried to tell you, but you would not see it, but now it is all explained.'

'How dare you speak to me so, miss! It is all your fault, I tell you. I brought you here specially to divert Sir Lionel's attention, but you have been useless. Useless! I wish I had never asked you to come. I should have encouraged Miss Gadsby, who would have been glad enough to have him, heaven knows, but I thought of my dear boy, and how it would be best to keep all the money in the family—*and* I thought to rescue you from a life of poverty and mediocrity, miss! And now see how my thoughtfulness is returned. I am to have Lady Ball for my niece-in-law, and taking precedence of me!'

'When—when were Sir Lionel and Lady Ball united, ma'am?' Sophie dared to ask.

'They are on their way to Gretna now. They left this morning—this very morning. It is all here in this letter which Sir Lionel sent me from Barnet.' And Lady Knight flourished a letter which she had been clutching all this time. 'They could not wait for the banns—oh, no! And so they are gone off to Scotland like a pair of twittering lovebirds! I shall leave, of course. I shall not stay for their return.'

'Leave! But they can not mean to turn you out, ma'am!'

'Of course not! I would like to see her try—that snake in the grass—to turn *me* out! But I shall not stay, and neither will you. We will all leave as soon as we have our portmanteaux packed. I shall not stay to see another woman mistress here. We shall all come down to Mallowfield and stay with you, sir!'

And Lady Knight glared at Mr Moreton. 'It will be sadly dull, but the season is nearly over, and you must have *some* neighbourhood in Dorset, I collect!'

Sophie looked at her stepfather to see what he had to say about this invasion of his quiet home, but all he said was,

'You will be very welcome, ma'am.'

Lady Knight rose.

'I must go and rest now. This news has quite taken my strength away. I simply do not know how I shall be able to face the world this evening. To think that my life in society should end in this!'

And she went out of the room, and in a moment Sophie and Mr Moreton heard her calling for Yvette.

Mr Moreton smiled at Sophie.

'I suppose you did not meet with Sir Lionel and Lady Ball upon the road this morning?'

Sophie shook her head.

'I saw nothing of them, sir, but then I was quite occupied in looking for Camilla and Mr Martin.'

'And I expect the company you were with was exceedingly interesting also?' said Mr Moreton with a little smile.

To his consternation his stepdaughter let out a wail and flung herself against him.

'Oh, sir! When can we return to Mallowfield?'

'Return to Mallowfield! But I thought that you and Lord Netherton——'

'I shall never see Lord Netherton again,' wept Sophie.

'Never see him again! What do you mean, my dear? What nonsense is this?'

'Oh, sir,' sobbed Sophie into Mr Moreton's chest, 'I—I *told* him I never wished to see him again! And—and—he—he—left!'

'Why ever did you do that, Sophie? I made sure that everything was now arranged between you.'

Sophie shook her head vigorously.

'I—I told him he was a b—b—brute and a ph—ph—philanderer, and that he was no gentleman!'

'Good gracious!' exclaimed Mr Moreton. 'Did you have any justification for these accusations?'

'Mr—Mr Martin mentioned that he had been pursuing a Miss W—W—Woodville all last season, but that he had not money enough to attach her.'

'It seems to me that Mr Martin is an even more foolish young man than I thought at first!'

'And—it was not a very gentlemanly thing to deceive me as he did!'

'Oh, dear; then I suppose you have not yet forgiven me for being an accomplice!'

'Of course I have, sir,' said Sophie dolefully, 'though why you should do it I can not conceive! But—Lord Netherton—and a philanderer on top of all!'

'But, my dear Sophie,' Mr Moreton began reasonably, 'Lord Netherton did not know you last year! You could not expect him not to dance at balls while waiting for you to appear—especially when he did not even know of your existence!'

'It is not that!' cried Sophie; 'he—he *pursued* her, and if she would have had him, he would not be——' She stopped abruptly.

'Yes?'

'He would not have been p—playing tricks on *me* now!' answered Sophie in a very small voice.

'I do not think Lord Netherton is playing any tricks, Sophie,' Mr Moreton said very gravely.

Sophie looked up into her stepfather's face, a little hope showing in her eyes. 'Do not you, sir?' she whispered.

Mr Moreton shook his head.

'Oh, but I have sent him away!' Sophie wailed anew. 'I shall never see him again! I—I tried to—to strike him!'

'And why did you do that?'

'I thought he was laughing at me,' Sophie sniffled.

'And I suppose you—you had—er—lost your temper?' Mr Moreton asked, suppressing a smile.

Sophie nodded.

'Oh, sir, what shall I do? I—I know how awful I must

look—I saw Lady Knight just now, and it suddenly struck me that *I* might look like that, and I could not bear it! And Lord Netherton has seen me so also, and I know I shall never see him again!'

And Sophie wept afresh.

'I do not think that things are as bad as you think, my dear,' said Mr Moreton, patting her shoulder. 'But in any case, some good may have come out of it if it teaches you that—that tantrums are not at all attractive.'

'Oh, sir,' cried Sophie looking up with a very tear-stained face, 'I will never lose my temper again, I swear it! But,' she added in a whisper, 'I *do* think I have been very ill-used!'

'I am sure Lord Netherton has a most satisfactory explanation, Sophie.'

'But I may never hear it, sir!'

'I think there is little doubt of that,' Mr Moreton answered kindly. 'But now, if we are not to be late for Mrs Darrington-ffinch's ball, I think we had better start preparing ourselves.'

'Oh, I could not go out this evening, sir!'

'Why ever not?'

'I have the headache! And in any case——'

And Sophie looked at her stepfather with huge, woebegone eyes.

'My dear Sophie, that simply is not true! No one, except Lord Netherton and his sister and myself, knows what has occurred, and I know that you may rely on their discretion, as—I hope—you know that you may rely on mine. And you can not shut yourself away for the rest of your life!'

Sophie looked unhappily at the floor but said nothing.

'After all,' Mr Moreton went on, 'your season is to be cut short; it would be a pity not to make the best of what remains.'

'But—but I might meet Lord Netherton!'

'And if you do, then you may apologise to each other,' said Mr Moreton, gently chiding. 'Come, Sophie my dear, you must make the effort.'

Sophie could not answer, except with a loud sniff.

In the event she saw neither Lord Netherton nor his sister that evening.

The following morning Sophie rose late after a sleepless night, her heart as heavy as ever. She wandered about the house, moving from room to room, unable to settle to anything. She caught sight of her face in one of the looking-glasses she passed, but had not the heart to raise her hand to pinch her cheeks into a little more life. Her grandmother and her stepfather were nowhere to be found, and she felt abandoned to her despair.

She wandered into the library and picked out a book illustrated with engravings of birds. She turned the pages absent-mindedly, but when she came to a plate illustrating the very species which had fallen at her feet when she was travelling to London with the erstwhile Mr Fanshawe, she could not hold back her tears.

It was at that moment that the doorbell pealed very loudly. She heard footsteps crossing the hall, then the sound of anxious voices. Sophie was so absorbed in her unhappiness that she took no notice, the fact that the servants were exhibiting less than their usual well-trained silence not even impinging upon her consciousness. In a moment, however, the door opened and Vickers, the butler, appeared, followed by two footmen carrying someone.

The little procession stopped and Sophie looked up to see what was happening. All she could see of the prone figure was a pair of highly polished boots.

'I beg your pardon, miss,' Vickers said, 'but I had thought the library unoccupied. The gentleman has—er—collapsed, miss, and I thought a library sofa the most convenient on which to place him. However, as you are here, miss, we will take the gentleman elsewhere.'

And Vickers gave a signal, and the highly polished boots started to disappear again.

'No, no, Vickers, I can go. It will be much the most convenient for the gentleman to be put here.'

'Very good, miss.'

Sophie began to move to the door and stared at the boots as they reappeared. In a moment the whole person of the recumbent figure was revealed. Sophie's face went white.

It was Lord Netherton being carried in by Thomas and Albert, his face as ashen as his stock.

The footmen put his lordship down on one of the long leather sofas and stood back, awaiting further orders. With a little strangled shriek Sophie ran forward and fell on her knees beside the prone Earl of Netherton.

'Mr Fanshawe! Dear Mr Fanshawe!' she cried. 'In the name of God, what has happened?'

And she turned round to look wildly at Vickers.

'His – er – lordship's horse threw him, miss, I understand. He collapsed as Thomas opened the door to him.'

'Oh!' cried Sophie frantically, turning back to the supine figure. 'Bring me some feathers! Fetch a doctor! His back may be broken!'

She took her handkerchief from her pocket and wiped the pale brow tenderly.

'Hurry! Hurry!' she cried. 'Oh, Vickers, what shall I do? His lordship may be dying! See how pale he is!'

In a few moments Thomas was back and handing her some burnt feathers and Sophie held them to Lord Netherton's nose.

'His eyelids moved, did you see, Vickers!' she cried delightedly.

'It seems his lordship's senses are indeed returning, miss.'

Lord Netherton's eyes now flickered open for a moment.

'Miss Neville!' he murmured, and closed them again with a great sigh.

'Oh, how are you, sir? Do you feel better, now?'

His lordship nodded his head slowly once or twice.

'How did this happen, sir? Were you indeed cast by your horse?' Sophie looked at the figure anxiously. 'Are you in great pain, sir?'

For answer his lordship groaned.

'Oh, why does not Dr Andrews come? Vickers, has he been sent for? Tell him it is most urgent! A man may be dying! Hurry, Vickers, hurry!'

'Albert has already summoned the doctor, miss,' replied the butler.

'There is no need,' whispered the Earl, and groaned again.

'But you are injured! We must have help!' Sophie peered down anxiously into the pale face. 'Tell me where it hurts. Let me put a cushion——'

'No,' gasped Lord Netherton, 'I am very well as I am. Just stay near me. Give me your hand. It comforts me.'

A spasm of pain crossed his features.

Sophie looked round frantically and saw that the room was suddenly quite empty but for themselves.

'Just—just smooth my forehead,' Lord Netherton said in feeble tones, 'that is all I can bear.'

Sophie wiped the pale face again with her handkerchief. A little colour seemed to come back into his countenance.

'I—I came, Miss Neville,' his lordship panted, scarcely above a whisper, 'I came to—to beg your forgiveness.' And he relapsed into silence again, his strength apparently quickly gone.

'And I must beg yours, sir,' Sophie whispered tenderly, tears welling up again in her eyes.

'You *do* forgive me then, Miss Neville?' the Earl gasped, before another spasm of pain twitched his features. 'I know you told me never to darken your doors again, but I *had* to see you once more. I had to speak with you. The consciousness of how ill I had treated you was too much for me to bear. Say you forgive me now, Miss Neville! Say I am forgiven before I go!'

'Go, sir?'

There was a small nod. 'I may not last long, Miss Neville. Give me the balm of your forgiveness now.'

'Of course I give it to you, sir,' Sophie whispered, blushing very pink as she said it, and wishing that medical aid would appear.

'Freely?' gasped the stricken man.

Sophie nodded, even though the eyes were still closed. 'Freely, my lord.'

'With all your heart, Miss Neville?'

'With all my heart, my lord.'

'Miss Woodville was of absolutely no importance,' the Earl insisted with an effort. 'You believe that, Miss Neville?'

'Yes, my lord,' Sophie whispered.

The Earl's bright blue eyes suddenly opened wide and stared up into her face. She blushed again.

'You have given me great comfort, Miss Neville,' he said smiling. Then his face creased with pain once more.

'Oh! I will fetch Dr Andrews myself! I can not think what he can be about!' cried Sophie, fearing that Lord Netherton was slipping away before her eyes.

She tried to rise to her feet, but the earl gripped her hand tightly. 'No, do not leave me!' he gasped. 'I cannot bear to be alone.'

Sophie stared at him. Lord Netherton had closed his eyes again. He *did* look very pale, and a fall from a horse could be fatal. If only Dr Andrews would come! She remembered with a heavy heart how a certain Mrs Gage in Mallowfield had been thrown from her horse and had suffered a broken neck. Tears sprang up again in her eyes, and spilled down her cheeks as she gazed tragically at the figure on the sofa.

A tear fell on to Lord Netherton's face. In a trice his eyes opened and he gazed for a moment at Sophie's tear-stained face above him. In a flash he was sitting upright and had put his arms about her.

'Sophie! Dearest, dearest Sophie!' he cried. 'Do not weep, my love; I can not bear it!'

Sophie stared at him for a moment, then began to struggle to push him away.

'Oh, it is monstrous, sir! Oh, how dare you!' she gasped. 'You have deceived me again! You have not finished with your games after all! How can you! How can you! It is a great deal too bad!'

'When you sent me away, I feared that unless I could touch your heart, you would indeed never speak to me again.'

'So you resorted to this—this charade!'

Lord Netherton nodded, looking suitably ashamed. 'I was afraid my crime was too great for forgiveness!'

'So you make it worse by more deceit!'

'You have forgiven me once; can you not again?'

'It was a forgiveness got by cheating! I take it back!'

'Sophie, Sophie, my love,' he said against her hair, 'do not be angry with me again, I beg you. Hurry up and forgive me this too, as you have forgiven Mr Fanshawe—and Miss Woodville—and then we can be comfortable again.'

Sophie struggled with all her might to push him away, but his arms seemed like iron bands about her, and she could hardly breathe, let alone move.

'Comfortable!' she managed to gasp. 'How dare you, sir! Let me go! Let me *go*!' she cried frantically, but her efforts were weak against the force of his embrace.

'Sophie, my love,' he murmured again.

At last she lay still in his arms and heaved a shuddering sigh. 'I do not see how I can ever forgive you this too,' she whispered.

'You have only to say, "I forgive you, dearest Michael",' he whispered back.

'"Dearest——!"' she repeated. 'What did you say?' she said, pushing herself back to look at his face.

'I said, "You have only to say—I forgive you, dearest Michael"—that is all,' he answered, smiling down at her with his incredibly blue eyes.

'All! All!'

He nodded. 'It is very easy. Repeat it after me. 'I forgive——'

'It does not seem to me, sir,' said Sophie with a frown, 'that you have any right to speak to me in such a fashion—or to hold me so,' she added, glancing down at his arms, which were around her still.

'I had not come here today only to beg your forgiveness, my love,' he began.

'Miss Neville,' Sophie corrected him.

'Miss Neville,' he amended.

'For what other purpose were you come, sir?'

'I had come, *Miss Neville*, intending to ask you to marry me.'

Sophie's smile of pure joy illumined her whole being.

'You could ask me now, sir,' she pointed out.

'So I could,' he agreed.

'Well?' she prompted, waiting.

'I am not sure that I like to, uncertain as I am of your answer. You have still not forgiven me.'

Sophie pursed her lips. She glanced down at Lord Netherton's hands still holding her elbows.

'I am not at all sure, sir, that I am in any position to refuse it.'

'Oh, Sophie!' he said, and drew her to him.

Sophie pushed his lordship away.

'I, too, sir, like to have things absolutely clear,' she said pointedly.

Lord Netherton smiled at her and he said with a laugh in his voice, 'Miss Neville, I am entirely yours, body and soul.'

Then suddenly the smile left his face, and kneeling at her side, he took her hands in his and said in a voice of great earnestness,

'I love you, dearest Sophie—everything about you—from your mightiest tantrum to the last fiery hair on your head! I could not live with a tame woman, my love: she would bore me to death in half an hour. But with you—with you I am never bored, whether you are trailing along behind a cart in a bedraggled dress, or sitting demurely in Mallowfield church pretending not to notice me. I want nothing more,' he went on, stifling Sophie's attempted protest, 'than to live the rest of my life beside you. And—if you will not marry me, Miss Neville,' he went on in mock despair, 'I shall—I shall go and shoot myself!' He smiled up at her.

'I could not have my—my cousin's blood on my conscience,' Sophie whispered, smiling tremulously and much moved.

'Oh, my dearest Sophie,' breathed Lord Netherton, and took her in his arms, 'tell me that you love me. Let me hear you say it—cousin!'

With shining eyes and with her heart on her lips, Sophie replied, 'I love you, Mr Fanshawe.'

And then Lord Netherton kissed her, and they did not speak again for some little time.

CHAPTER
FOURTEEN

SOME while later, when her head was resting on his shoulder and they were indeed comfortable again, Sophie, thinking over all that had happened, suddenly said reproachfully, 'It really was too bad of you—coming to Mallowfield like that—to look me over!'

'What *do* you mean?' he cried, much astonished.

'My stepfather, Mr Moreton, wished me to be engaged before my come-out: he was so afraid of the people I would meet here at my grandmamma's house—and in one instance, at least, I must say, he was quite right. So he looked about for a suitor for me, and discussed the matter with his friend, Sir Llewellyn Godfrey, who was an old friend of your uncle's, or so I collect, and then—but you know all this as well as I do. There you suddenly were, in Mallowfield church! Now, if you did *not* come to look me over, I should like to know what *did* bring you there, sir!' Her eyes flashed, and she looked pinkly indignant.

'My dearest girl, I assure you I did no such thing! I came down to stay with my friend Barton in order to inspect my new estates: I have land near Mallowfield, but the house is fallen into ruin. I swear I had not heard of you till I came into Dorset; but when I did see you, I determined to marry you at once!'

'Did you really?' Sophie whispered, wanting to believe him, but hardly daring to.

'Certainly I did!' Lord Netherton said very firmly. 'Why else should I have come to Mallowfield church? Not to look you over, but to bask in your nearness. I had seen you driving and had asked Barton who you were. He told me he thought you were still in the schoolroom, though I must say it did not seem very likely to me. And of course I was delighted when I met your stepfather, Mr Moreton. But that is why I attended Mallowfield church; not merely to escape the fire and brimstone preaching of Mr Fenton, though I was glad enough to do that.'

'But why did not you tell me who you were when we were on the road to London? You had plenty of opportunity then. You might have told me then that you had met Mr Moreton!'

'Ah! Now that is a little more difficult to explain. I suppose there are several reasons,' Lord Netherton returned thoughtfully.

'And what are they?' asked Sophie, hoping for more compliments.

'When Mr Moreton informed me on my arrival at Mallowfield—punctual to the moment, I may add!—that you had dashed off, he knew not where, positively refusing even to meet me, I confess I was extremely surprised and intrigued. No young lady—and I hope I do not sound conceited as I say this, but I assure you it is the exact truth—no young lady had ever run away from me so precipitately before, and I saw at once that, not only were you beautiful, but also a young woman of spirit and independence—and that interested me. Now, when we met, if I had approached you and said: "I am Netherton", you might quite well have refused to speak to me.'

'I do not think that likely,' Sophie said softly.

'Nevertheless, it was a risk. You see, I did not know about my supposed baldness and senility then,' he said with an amused smile. 'And when I did actually meet with you—and I may say my calculations went awry at first and I missed you entirely—I am so glad you did not have to pass that night in a hayloft, for you did not seem very adept at finding a proper bed-chamber for yourself!'—and here Lord Netherton leaned backwards as Sophie pretended to hammer him with

her fists in mock rage—'well, when I did meet with you, I
say, you appeared to me to be a young lady who would like
an—adventure. Your hat betrayed you at once, you know; it
was an excessively dramatic one!'

'I thought so too, at the time,' laughed Sophie, remembering the bedraggled green monstrosity which had finished its
life in a roadside ditch.

'When it became clear that you had not the first idea who I
was, I determined to leave you in ignorance for a while.
Though it *was* very hard at times!'

'You should have been quite open with me!'

'I know, I know. But when you informed me that I was
bald and tottering on the brink of my grave, I did not quite
know how I *could* make my revelation!'

Sophie smiled broadly at this. 'You did look somewhat
taken aback, I remember!'

'I was astonished, my love!' He looked at her severely. 'I
cannot think *where* you gained such an idea!'

'Well, I am very glad that you are not bald!' she cried,
laughing.

'So am I!'

'And had you yet further reasons for practising your gross
deception upon me?' his love enquired.

'Confess, first,' Lord Netherton smiled, 'that it was not
wholly unpleasant.'

'It was all *quite* disgraceful, sir! And had your calculations
continued to go awry, I might have had to starve!'

'Never! I should have arrived in time. I could not possibly
have let my future wife want for anything. She was already
far too precious to me.' And he kissed the tip of Sophie's nose.

'Now, come, confess, was not it a great deal of fun? Did not
you feel the least little bit like a heroine? Leonore, perhaps?'

'I will admit nothing, sir!'

'Are not you at all pleased that I hastened after you? That I
could not bear to let my future wife out of my sight?'

'I should hate you, sir!'

'But you do not.'

Sophie laughed and shook her head fondly. 'You are the outside of enough!'

And then she made it quite plain that she was very glad that his lordship had acted as he did.

'And have you confessed everything now, sir?' she asked some time later. 'For I should be very glad to know that all deception was quite over between us.' She smiled up into Lord Netherton's face. 'I could not bear it if all were *not* comfortable about us.'

'And neither could I, my love,' the Earl responded eagerly. 'So I will confess my last—most terrible reason.'

'Terrible?'

'I—I thought—it—occurred to me—that it would be an excellent way to find out if—if you would love me for myself, and not just for—for my new title—and—and my money. You can not conceive,' he went on hurriedly as Sophie was about to protest hotly, 'how very disagreeable these last few months have been. Before I became rich—during our last season—there were a great many matrons in society who positively refused to put me on their list, and who would not send my sister a card for their balls. We were not grand enough for them then, you see. But this year I have been chased by every mamma, I think, who has an unmarried daughter anywhere within ten years of my age—on either side! Including a rather formidable matron near Mallowfield, with a young daughter of about your age. Happily the young lady has her interests engaged elsewhere.'

'Poor Lady Hetherington!' Sophie giggled. 'I am afraid she is sadly disappointed in Camilla. And so,' she went on, trying to sound severe, 'you have been much chased, sir?'

'You would not believe it!'

'And what happened to Miss Woodville?'

'Ah!' said Lord Netherton significantly. 'To tell you the exact truth, Miss Neville, she suddenly became exceedingly charming, but *I* did not find the lady quite so—desirable—after all!'

'I am very glad to hear it! But are you so *very* rich?'

'I am afraid I am. Do you mind?'

Sophie shook her head. 'You really have treated me very badly, you know!'

'But you have forgiven me, my dearest.'

'You do not at all deserve it, sir, but I am afraid I have!' She bent over to kiss Lord Netherton's cheek, and then stood up. 'But now I think we should look for my stepfather. I think he will like to know that I find Mr Netherton much to my liking after all.'

They found Mr Moreton reading the daily newspaper in the small salon. He looked up expectantly as they came in.

'I—I thought you would like to know, sir,' Sophie began, suddenly feeling a little shy, 'that I will now be very glad indeed to fall in with your original plans for me to—to marry—er—Mr Michael Netherton.'

And she held Lord Netherton's hand very tightly.

Mr Moreton was all smiles in a moment, and embraced Sophie and shook the Earl warmly by the hand. 'I am so very happy,' he cried. 'My dear Sophie—your lordship——'

'Oh, please, sir, Michael,' put in his lordship.

'Michael,' repeated Mr Moreton, wiping his eyes without pretence, 'nothing could give me greater pleasure!'

'I quite agree with you,' said Sophie, smiling fondly at *her* Mr Fanshawe.

'I always knew it was an excellent idea,' Mr Moreton said.

'Now I come to think of it, my lord,' said Sophie, turning with shining eyes to the Earl, 'it was Mr Moreton who quite distinctly said that you were old and bald. I remember the occasion exactly. We have very much to blame him for—keeping us apart for so long!'

'Did you indeed say that, sir?' asked the Earl, severely astonished.

'I protest I never said any such thing! In fact I know

positively I *never* mentioned any absence of hair! I merely intimated, sir, that you were a *few* years older than Sophie. Nothing more. It was Sophie's own imagination that supplied all the rest.'

'Or *The Prisoner of the Vampire*,' the Earl suggested with a smile.

Sophie blushed, but said loftily, 'There *were* quite remarkable coincidences, as you yourself remarked, my lord. By the way, do you have my book? I confess I should quite like to know how Leonore's story ends.'

The Earl assured her that he had kept it safely, but their further conversation was halted by the sudden arrival of Lady Knight, who flung open the door and sailed into the room, her auburn curls bobbing and her face wreathed in smiles. His grace, the Duke of Mayfair, followed her at a slower pace.

'I have first to tell you,' Lady Knight cried, addressing Mr Moreton, 'that Sophie and I will not, after all, be coming to Mallowfield, sir. It was so kind of you to extend such a warm invitation, in the terrible circumstances in which I then found myself, but happily it is not now necessary. I may have to leave this house,' she cried dramatically, 'but I shall still have a roof—a far better roof—over my head.'

She stopped and saw Lord Netherton for the first time.

'I am delighted to see you here, my lord, I did not know that you were come. Sophie, my dear, perhaps you would like to show his lordship the new roses in the courtyard? The stock came directly from Malmaison, sir. King Louis promised me some plants when he was in London before his restoration, and they have but recently arrived. I am sure you will be interested to see them, my lord.'

'I am quite certain that his lordship will be delighted to be shown them by Sophie,' Mr Moreton agreed, 'but first I have some news to tell you. Lady Knight, Your Grace, I have given my consent to the betrothal of Sophie and the Earl of Netherton.'

'Oh!' For a moment Lady Knight was too astonished to speak. Then she flew to Sophie and put her arms round her. 'Darling child!' she cried, 'I am so happy for you. How clever you have been,' she went on in a whisper as she was embracing Sophie, 'you need not now bother to show his lordship those boring roses after all!'

Meanwhile the Duke of Mayfair was enthusiastically shaking the Earl's hand and beaming at him.

'Well done, my boy; you could not have hit upon a more delightful bride in all London!'

'I am very glad you approve, sir!' said his lordship.

'Your father, I know, would be delighted, were he here, and your dear mother also. I certainly give you my blessing. Well, Miss Sophie, so you are to be my god-daughter-in-law?'

'I did not know that——' Sophie cried, looking at Lord Netherton.

'I think I mentioned that his grace is our near neighbour in Berkshire,' the Earl said. 'Well, he is my godfather.'

'*And* his grace will be connected with you, Sophie, in an even more familiar way, will you not, my love,' cried Lady Knight, slipping her arm through the Duke's.

'My love!' cried three pairs of lips in united astonishment.

'That is why Lady Knight need not impose upon you at Mallowfield, sir,' the Duke said smiling to Mr Moreton. Then he patted Lady Knight's hand and said to them all, 'My old friend has agreed to make me the happiest man in the world,' he said proudly, and the two old people smiled at each other with genuine affection.

The exclamations of surprise from the hearers were not soon hushed, and there was a great deal more kissing and hand-shaking and mutual congratulations.

'And I shall not, after all,' Lady Knight said triumphantly, and with a great deal of thankfulness, 'have to give place to that odious creature, Lady Ball. How very furious she will be! Now I come to think of it, though, I am really quite glad that she has got her claws into Lionel, for otherwise I do not think that it would have occurred to someone to make me a Duchess!'

She smiled up at the Duke, and he whispered to Sophie, 'I think I once told you, my dear, that the London season was not only designed to give pleasure to the young!'

A footman entered at this moment to announce a caller.

'It is Miss Fanshawe, my lady, asking for his lordship. Miss Fanshawe instructed me to enquire of his lordship, my lady,' Thomas went on without a trace of a smile, 'if she had timed it correctly, because if she is come too soon, Miss Fanshawe says that she can perfectly well go away again and come back later when all is settled, my lady.'

Sophie broke into a peal of laughter.

'Pray tell Miss Fanshawe that she is come at *exactly* the right moment,' she said. 'And that we shall be with her in a moment.'

The footman retired, and she turned to Lord Netherton.

'I think I shall like my new sister a great deal after all!' she cried. 'Come, Michael, let us go and meet her together and you can present us again, and we can begin anew. After all, we have a great deal more in common now than just our red hair!'

Sophie never bothered to finish reading *The Prisoner of the Vampire*, even though Lord Netherton had kept it most safely for her. But she did just peep at the end.

Of course Leonore ended safe in the arms of the Prince of Gurgglesbuttel von Wittgenstein zu Schwarzfeldt—just as Sophie herself had ended safe in Lord Netherton's arms. Heroines, after all, always got their heroes—otherwise they would not be heroines. Sophie smiled contentedly. It was so much more exciting to *be* a heroine than to read about them. And she was to be married within the six months she had originally specified to Mr Moreton. Oh, yes! It was very satisfactory being a heroine!

Masquerade
Historical Romances

Intrigue
excitement
romance

Don't miss
April's
other enthralling Historical Romance title

GLEN OF FROST
by Belinda Grey

Duncan, Laird of Clan Seidhe, has two sons: Lachlan, the legitimate heir, is reckless, generous and a devoted follower of the king, while Jamie, his bastard brother, cares for nothing but his own gain. The only thing the brothers share is their orphaned cousin, Fiona, who is caught in their bitter struggle when, loving Lachlan, she is forced to marry the cold-hearted Jamie, The feud, begun in 1736 between children in a Scottish glen, reaches a terrible climax at the infamous Battle of Culloden where the half-brothers fight on opposing sides to decide the fate of the Stuart cause.

Masquerade
Historical Romances

Intrigue
excitement
romance

THE FLAME STONE
by Kate Buchan

Charlotte's return to her childhood home in France was far from happy. In her absence her father had been branded a traitor, and Etienne de Chatigny — the man she loved — had married another girl. But why was the old Count so hated? And why did Etienne behave as though Charlotte had deserted *him*?

A GIFT FOR PAMELA
by Judy Turner

Lord Crispin O'Neill had forgotten to buy a gift for Miss Pamela Courtney, so he felt he had every reason for buying Peri — a most unusual slave girl — to repair his omission. Unfortunately, Miss Courtney loathed Peri on sight, and his lordship had to revise his plans in a hurry!

Look out for these titles in your local paperback shop from 8th May 1981

Masquerade
Historical Romances

Intrigue
excitement
romance

CHANGE OF HEART
by Margaret Eastvale

Edmund, Lord Ashorne, returned from the
Peninsular Wars to find that his fiancée had married
his cousin. It was her sister Anne who had remained
single for his sake!

LION OF LANGUEDOC
by Margaret Pemberton

Accused of witchcraft by Louis XIV's fanatical
Inquisitor, Marietta was rescued by Léon de
Villeneuve — the Lion of Languedoc. How could she
not fall in love with him, even knowing that he
loved another woman?

These titles are still available through your local paperback
retailer